Ruthless

Vi Carter

Contents

Other Books by VI CARTER

Other Books by VI CARTER

<u>MURPHY'S MAFIA MADE MEN</u>
SINNER'S VOW #1
SAVAGE MARRIAGE #2

<u>YOUNG IRISH REBELS SERIES</u>
MAFIA PRINCE #1
MAFIA KING #2
MAFIA GAMES #3
MAFIA BOSS #4

<u>WILD IRISH SERIES</u>
FATHER (PREQUEL)

VICIOUS #1
RECKLESS #2
RUTHLESS #3
FEARLESS #4
HEARTLESS #5

<u>THE BOYNE CLUB</u>
DARK #1
DARKER # 2
DARKEST #3
PITCH BLACK #4

THE OBSESSED DUET
A DEADLY OBSESSION #1
A CRUEL CONFESSION #2

BROKEN PEOPLE DUET
BREAK ME #1
SAVE ME #2

CHAPTER ONE

CONNOR

F EAR. I CAN TASTE it on my tongue. My heavy limbs move from side to side, shuffling. My body tells my brain that I need to stay warm against the harsh cold. My hammering heart wants me to leave. My feet glide back slightly, and a weakness has me blinking rapidly. A voice inside my head warns me away from this fight as my eyes take in the crowd that pulsates around me.

Men wearing woolly hats, their hands shoved into pockets, huddle in a large circle around me. Their heavy jackets and warm clothing are not enough to keep the sharp cold out.

I want to feel the pain that accompanies the bitter cold, but I don't. I only feel fear. My opponent moves around the circle, arms outstretched as his fingers flex, enticing the crowd to feed off his energy. His bare back is covered in acne, the steroids pushing his body to places it shouldn't be pushed.

A young boy, maybe sixteen, holds up his phone in my opponent's face as he roars into the screen. Muscles straining, veins bulging. I remember that feeling myself. That sense of power. That sense of invisibility. Now I just do it to feel something.

We both wear only tracksuit bottoms. My feet continue to shuffle back and forth on their own accord. The field we stand in is already moist from last night's downpour, and my small and consistent movements are making the ground under my feet slippery. I move with lead feet, my mind once again roaring for me to leave this circle of men.

Rick enters the circle. He glances at me and gives me a quick nod. His red tracksuit is stark in the sea of black clothing. The crowd seems quieter now. My heart pounds in my ears. I'm aware now of all the eyes on me, aware of cold air. It's starting to bite my skin. I enjoy the moment of pain. Rick rubs his hands together, his eyes glowing with excitement. He enjoys the fights, but he loves the money more.

"Okay, lads, let's get started." My opponent and Rick move closer to me. I keep my eyes focused on the ground. I'm sure if I look up and into his eyes, I won't fight him.

"No biting. We aren't animals." A roar goes up as Rick lists out the rules. "No hanging on to each other. You want someone to hang on to, go to your mother's tit."

I nod mechanically. Rick's hand circles my closed fist; the contact of his warmth on my freezing skin makes me glance up at him.

"The balls are off-limits and an immediate disqualification."

I nod to Rick, and my eyes flicker to the pumped-up guy I'm fighting. He smashes his fists together and bounces on his feet. He's on something. His pupils are dilated, and that gives me some peace. The fear in me dilutes. Maybe he won't feel what I'm about to unleash on him.

"Fight!" Rick shouts as he disappears into the roaring crowd. We're far enough away from the main road to go unheard. There's nothing but cows in the near fields and a tire center at our backs. Rick owns the tire center, and I work there for him.

My opponent charges me, and I move quickly to the left. It's that movement that has everything slamming back into me. The time, the noise, the feeling—my whole body feels like it's on fire with the cold.

I turn as he charges me again, and I clothesline him. He's on his back, and his whole body tenses as he tries to catch his breath. Rick moves to the front of the crowd, ready to step in, but he knows I won't attack a man when he's down. Instead, I walk the circle as I wait. I keep my eyes trained on the ground and ignore the roars of the surrounding men. When I do look up, my father's face is there in all the men who roar at me, demanding blood. Demanding that I attack. I blink rapidly as my eyes leave the men and return to the boy on the ground.

He gets up swiftly. He roars again, pumping up the crowd. He's bouncing on his feet like a real boxer and craning his neck from side to side before he rushes me. I clench my fists and wait until he's there. There's a satisfaction when the skin on my knuckles splits with the impact of the first punch I land to his jaw. My aching hands want me to stop, but if I stop now, it will make the second and third punch more painful on me, so I keep hitting him in succession until he topples to the ground again.

As I wait, I push the image of my father out of my mind and focus on my brother, Shane. He hates bare-knuckle fighting, said we should leave it to the travelers and low-lifes. "We are the low-lifes," I would tell him, and his laugh would be filled with hate and a want to hurt me. But in a fight, I would win. Shane always thought of other ways to hurt me. Having money didn't make someone a better person. Shane thought it did. He acted like he was above everyone else. Even the law.

The boy gets up, his face a bloody mess. He bounces again on his feet, but the energy he showed earlier is nearly gone. He doesn't roar into the crowd either. He's a little smarter now when he waits for me to come to him, and one thing about me is I won't keep him waiting. Yet I'm not ready to end this fight. So I move too closely; my foot looks like it falters, causing me to push my hands out and away from my face. It's the opening I offer him. Our eyes meet, and he knows. But he's smart, so he takes it.

Pain races down the side of my face. I push it away and don't focus on it, not allowing him to get two in. I turn, and my fist rises faster than his, connecting with his chin. My skin tears further from the impact as he stumbles away from me. I don't want to stop, so I quickly move to him. His outstretched hands and the way his body twists away from me, like it's trying to protect itself, stops me from hitting him further.

"I'm done," he says along with a dribble of red spit. Rick is there, his red tracksuit filling my vision. He dyed his hair again, this time a dark black. I want to tell him it looks fake. He takes my wounded fist in his. The bite of pain has me closing my eyes as he declares me the winner. I don't look at the men who start to disperse. The cold and the lack of entertainment will drive them all home.

I take the few steps away from everyone as I grab my bag. I take out a T-shirt and hoodie and pull them over my damp skin.

"You free next Saturday night?"

I glance at Rick. He's bouncing now. My eyes are drawn to his white runners before shooting up to his gaze. "Not if you're going to keep giving me jumped-up kids." I slug the bag across my back, then take the money Rick holds out to me and stash it in my pocket.

"He was in his thirties," he says, stuffing his hands into his pockets. The air puffs around our words now. The noise of engines starting up has me glancing at the patch of grass the boy had sat down on after the fight. The same spot is now empty.

"Cocaine and steroids aren't a good mix, Rick."

"What do you want, Connor? You want me to test everyone who wants to fight you? You got your money, so what's the problem?" Rick narrows his eyes while running a hand through his hair.

I want to tell him it's not about the money, that it's about the thrill. But I don't. "Just try to have someone who isn't off their face next time." I pull my bag tighter against my back and Rick nods.

"Fine, I'll try. But it's getting harder to find people who will fight you."

I snort as I walk away. "Someone always wants to fight me, Rick."

"See you next Saturday," he roars as I make my way onto the main road. I take a left at Cassidy's cross. I'm staying only a few miles away from our fight spot, in a restaurant that has some outbuildings for B&Bs. It's clean, and no one knows me. Just the way I like it. I've been staying at the Cross Guns. It's the longest I've ever dared to stay in one spot.

I remember watching a wildlife documentary and the phrase "moving is life" stuck with me, and it's a code I try to live by. But recently, I've tired of running. I've gotten a job at the tire center, helping out with fixing cars. Money is shit, but what I get from fighting keeps me afloat. That's how I met Rick. He is a decent enough guy, if you minus the secondhand parts we charge full price for.

Lights move past me, and I move in toward the ditch until darkness consumes the road again. I walk with aching and bleeding hands stuffed in my pockets. The fight has released some tension that was bubbling up inside me. Seeing Una, my stepsister, walking into the Cross Guns a few weeks ago had terrified me, but once I discovered she was alone, I relaxed with her.

We always got on, and she hadn't seen the family in months and promised she wouldn't tell. But I knew I would have to move on soon. Secrets never stay buried for long with our family. Eventually, they will find out where I am.

It takes me thirty minutes before the lights of the Cross Guns come into view. I jog out back and go straight to my room. My single bed faces the door, freshly made. The room looks bare; I don't have anything, only clothes that are stacked neatly in the wardrobe.

I switch on the TV and mute it but let the light flicker across the room as I enter the adjoining bathroom. I don't linger in the shower but let the hot water warm me up before I patch up my fists. I tape them up mechanically as I watch the news reporter deliver some news about war in a foreign country. Buildings stand partially erect, rubble and crying people roam around the news reporter. After switching the TV off, I get dressed.

Stuffing some fifty euro notes into my jeans pocket, I put on a clean shirt before looking at myself in the mirror for the first time. I've a small red mark on my jaw—it's nothing much. I normally would never allow someone to get a hit on me, but I needed something to release the energy that was bouncing around inside me.

Leaving the room, I make my way across the gravelled parking lot I enter the small cozy pub, which holds a few patrons. They all turn as I enter but dismiss me. We're all here every night. On the first night, they tried to strike up a conversation, and I kept it to a yes-no answer. Since then, they've left me alone. I sit at the end of the bar.

"A beer," I tell Simon, the barman. He wears a black T-shirt with a Guns N' Roses symbol on the front. His wrinkled and over-tanned skin hangs slightly. Long hair that should be shaved is thinning; his glory days are fading away quicker than he can grasp them.

Simon places the beer in front of me with a nod, and I slide him a fifty. Long manicured fingers stop Simon from taking my fifty.

"Allow me."

I know Simon is waiting for me to agree, so I look up stiffly and nod as my brother sits down beside me.

CHAPTER TWO

CONNOR

"I 'LL HAVE A JAMESON." Shane speaks clearly, and I can hear the smile in his voice. It's a polished smile, one that's forced and controlled.

I sip my pint, trying to calm my erratic heartbeat as my mind races through different scenarios. How is this going to work? He's here to take me home, or worse.

"How did you find me?" I ask after Simon places the drink in front of Shane. He shifts, and I look at him. My brother looks the exact same as he did two years ago. Only now, maybe there is a harder edge to his brown eyes. His face is clean shaven, and the black shirt and slacks makes him look ready to enter a business meeting. He wears the same silver band on his thumb that our mother bought him.

"Nice to see you too, brother," he says before taking a slow sip of his drink. His eyes never leave mine. He's angry, which doesn't surprise me, but the pretend smile that he keeps on his face does. He isn't one for hiding his emotions from me.

His eyes flicker to my knuckles, and the urge to hide them has me sitting still. "How did I find you? The notorious Connor O'Reagan fighting again. You made it too easy. I could have tracked you down months ago."

Yeah, I knew that fighting would draw them out. Maybe subconsciously I wanted this. That idea had me gripping my pint. I didn't want them. I didn't want this life. I never did.

"What do you want?"

Shane's smile slips, and he moves his stool closer to me.

"I want my brother to come home."

I'm shaking my head at his manipulative words.

"Did he send you?" I can't keep the bitterness from my voice, and Shane leans away from me, picking up his glass. He empties it before setting it back down on the bar. "No, Finn misses you."

Hearing my brother's name has my stomach twisting with guilt, and I stare at Shane again. "You didn't come here for Finn. You're a selfish bastard." I empty my pint as he laughs before standing. He follows me from the pub as I knew he would. Once the door is closed to my room, I turn to Shane.

"Look, just this once, can't you say you didn't find me?"

He isn't listening to me; his eyes are roaming my room. "You live here?" The horror in his voice gives me satisfaction, and when I don't answer him, he looks at me.

"Orders are to bring you home, brother, and I always complete my jobs."

I don't have to ask who sent the orders. I don't have to ask what will happen if I don't come.

Bastards.

I'm stuffing clothes into a bag when Shane stops me.

"I'll be outside." His pampered ass leaves my room. I don't linger. I don't tidy over before I follow my brother out into his blacked-out Jeep with my only bag of possessions.

Shane grins as I opt to sit in the back seat. The tinted windows dim the interior.

"I see that you're letting your guard down while fighting." Shane still wears the grin as he watches me in the rearview mirror.

"Is that how you found me?"

He glances at the road as he takes a right, but there's a tension in his shoulders at my question.

"Yeah," he finally lies, and I glare out the window, watching a dark version of the world go by. It doesn't take long for us to reach the house. Shane slows down at the front door, and I jump out, slugging my bag across my back. My eyes travel upward, the sheer size of the large white house something I could never get used to. Entering the house, I get the smell of beeswax and polish, and my stomach twists.

I kick the door closed behind me and head for the kitchen. Mary might be there, and she's worth seeing. The closer I get to the kitchen, the more I relax. I can smell pancakes. It's familiar. I inch the door open and both my brows rise.

"Una."

She screams and drops the spoon she was licking; it's covered in what looks like syrup.

"Connor." After picking up the spoon from the floor, she throws it onto the counter, grinning, and she closes the space between us. I hug her back as the back door opens. Shane's face stiffens. He wasn't expecting Una to be here. He never really liked her. She turns in my arms and smiles at him. It's not the grin she just gave me. She walks to him, and he's taking every inch of her in. My shock expands when she stands on her tippy toes and plants a kiss on his lips.

"You told them where I was," I say, and she faces me, heat scorching her cheeks.

"I'm sorry, Connor, but we all missed you."

I nod at her. That's the story they were selling her. I flicker a quick glance toward Shane, who's watching me.

"It's okay," I tell Una. She's sweet. She was always nice to me. What she's doing with Shane is beyond me.

Una untangles herself from Shane and bounces toward me, but she stops a foot away and leans against the counter. "So are you staying for long?" She's smiling, and I place my bag on the counter.

"I'm not sure," I tell her, and her smile widens.

"I was the same when I came here, and now they can't get rid of me." She says the last part while looking at Shane, who still hasn't stepped away from the back door. He's observing us, like he doesn't know what to make of this conversation. Because he's so uncomfortable, I decide to put on the kettle.

"Maybe you won't be able to get rid of me either," I tell her, and Una narrows her eyes slightly at me, but the smile is still visible. "Maybe we could watch all the movies we never got to," I tell her, and her gaze flickers to Shane. He's clenching his fists.

"I'd like that. I did actually watch *Rambo* and *Taken* recently."

Two of my favorites. "Without me?" I ask.

"You've been gone for a while," Shane says, and I snort a laugh at him.

"Shane," Una pleads, but I can't stop the smirk that grows slowly on my face.

"I can leave again," I tell him, pointing at the kitchen door, and he takes a few steps until he's close to Una.

"Unfortunately, that's not an option," he tells me, and Una's eyes widen.

"Shane, please."

It's funny to watch him squirm. His eyes shift around the kitchen as he plays with the band on his thumb.

"I need to have a word with Connor alone," he tells Una, his tone softer.

I make myself a cup of tea as Una defends me, and Shane gets wound up. It's funny to watch, and I enjoy it, until he promises her it's just a chat and we'll be back shortly. I raise both eyebrows while taking a sip of the tea and walking past Una.

"We'll catch up later," she tells me.

Shane takes us to the room where jobs were always delved out in. The bar is polished, and I sit at it with my cup of tea. When Shane joins me, I want to move, but I don't.

"So you and Una?" I question before taking another noisy drink of my tea. It always pissed Shane off, and I want to maximize that.

"I have a job for you." Shane rubs the bar counter as he speaks.

"Yeah?" I knew I was dragged home for a reason.

"A girl might have witnessed me hurting someone, and I want you to find out what she saw." Shane pulls a piece of paper from his pocket.

Another noisy gulp of my tea. "That's it?"

I take the piece of paper from Shane. *Ava Smith, Apartment Four, John Street Kells* is scrawled across it. I rise and stuff it into my back pocket before sitting back down.

"Yeah, but it's important, so don't fuck it up."

"I see you haven't lost your charm," I tell him, and he gets up.

"Report back to me."

"Not Michael?" I question, and he stares at me before answering.

"Me, Connor. Not Liam, not Michael. Me."

I don't respond, continuing to drink my tea. He thinks I'm the same boy he left here three years ago.

I'm not that boy anymore.

CHAPTER THREE

AVA

*T*HUMP, *THUMP, THUMP.*

I keep my eyes closed as my landlord continues to bang on my door. I keep still, hiding in my bedroom, my hand over my heart as he calls my name.

"Ava, I know you're in there."

Thump, thump, thump.

Oh God, just go away.

This is humiliating, and I want to slide down the wall to the floor, but I don't dare make a sound. I didn't think he saw me come in. I used the back door and was so quiet climbing the stairs to the second floor. The bottom one is occupied by a hairdresser and bookies. The rest of the building has four apartments. I made sure no one saw me, so how did he know I was here? I didn't turn on the TV, and my bare feet didn't make much noise on the floor.

"I'll be back, Ava!" he shouts before his steps descend the stairs. It's only now that I allow myself to slump down the wall until I sit on the coral-colored carpet. I sit and allow my heart to slow down and return to a normal beat.

The front door slams, and my eyes burn, but I don't let the tears run. I hate hiding. I hate being late with my rent, but lately, I've had no luck. The image of my nan with her small blue eyes and large nose makes me smile. If I told her what happened, she would either pay my bill or insist I come back to live with her. But that's not an option. Trouble has a habit of following me around, and that is something I refuse to bring to her door. She doesn't deserve that.

I get ready for work and pray to God, if he really exists, to let me just make it to work without meeting my landlord. I slip from my one-bed apartment and put the key into my gray jacket before taking a sprint down the stairs and out the back door.

The wind has picked up. It's only four in the afternoon and, already, the sky grows dark. I work two doors away from where I live, but I don't want to use the front door, so this way is a bit longer. It's a walk around the block. I hate it, as it's not lit up. Getting to work is fine. It's coming back that always has me walking with hunched shoulders.

I take out my phone to ring Nan, and she picks up on the third ring. "Birdy, I was wondering when you were going to ring me."

I smile into the phone as I duck my head down to avoid the wind in my eyes.

"I know, Nan. I was at the gym." I roll my eyes at the stupid lie, and her soft giggle makes me feel worse.

"I don't know what for. You know an empty bag won't stand."

I grin now. She says this all the time.

"And too full of a one won't bend," I counteract, and I can almost hear the smile.

"Will you be calling later?"

"I'm just heading into work, but I'll give you a call tomorrow. We can talk longer," I tell her, and her disappointment is evident in her tone.

"Okay, birdy. You take care of yourself."

"I love you, Nan." The doorway is littered with cigarette butts I will have to sweep up later. But right now, I just want to get out of the cold.

"Love you, too, birdy."

I say my goodbye as I enter the lounge, ready to stuff my jacket and phone behind the counter, but the room isn't empty like it normally is. My landlord, Sean, is waiting for me. He gives me the creeps. He drinks way too much, and his eyes have a habit of wandering. The apartment is a shit hole, but it's cheap. Even being so cheap, I'm still struggling.

"Ava, I was at your flat earlier." He grins as his eyes rake over me. The tight jeans and top are revealing, but I stand taller, not allowing him to think for one second that he's making me uncomfortable.

"You'll get your money, Sean." My sharp words have him glaring at me.

"I know I will, but..." He moves closer, the smell of alcohol nearly choking me. He looks like a hundred-year-old fisherman, his face weather-beaten. "I could think of other ways." He's so close to my face that I want to gag, but I don't flinch.

"You can keep *thinking*, but that's all it will ever be: a thought." I move around him and remove my jacket while trying to hide my trembling hands and stuff it under the counter. I turn around as his seven-foot frame approaches the counter. I'm glad the counter is between us. I pick up a cloth just to give myself something to do. I don't want to piss him off completely. I don't want to lose my job, but I don't want to appear weak either.

"I promise I'll have your money soon," I say, trying to remove some of the anger from his features. I wipe the clean counter. "What can I get you?"

"A whiskey that *you* will pay for."

I nod, hating that I have to do this, but if it buys me time, I'll consider it interest. I ring it up and stick the receipt into my pocket so I don't forget to pay for it later.

When I started working here at Smyth's pub, friends used to come in, always expecting a free drink, but they soon realized that wasn't going to happen. I pay for every drink I take myself or give away. There are no freebies, and the owner, Patrick, is such a decent guy that I would never do anything to jeopardize his business. It's already slow.

I give Sean his drink and don't even get a thank you, but I'm glad to get away from him. I enter the main bar. A few lads play pool, and pints of lager sit on the edge of the pool table. Paul, a nice guy and a local, grins up at me and gives me a nod.

"Pints off the table, lads," I say, and they remove them with mumbles of sorry. There isn't an ounce of harm in any of them. We live in a town with high unemployment and too many pubs. It causes young people like Paul and his friends to flock to the local pubs.

The door into the back is slightly open, and I push it open further to see Patrick tallying up receipts.

"Ava, you're in." A large smile accompanies his words.

My stomach flutters with what I want to ask, but I keep it calm. "Yep. Just Paul and the lads in, that's all."

He nods. "Yeah, if I didn't need the customers, I'd run them."

"They'd just go to another pub. You'd do no good."

"Maybe they'd decide to do something with their lives."

Not a chance, but I don't say that. "Maybe. I was wondering if there are any extra shifts going?"

Patrick looks guilty, and I want to take my words back. He hates saying no.

"I had to let Lindsey go."

"Ah, no. I'm sorry, Patrick. She was lovely. Look, it was just for extras, so no worries."

"Are you sure?" he asks, and I nod.

"I am." I smile wide. "I better get back to work before the boss sees me dossing," I say, and he laughs as I close the door. I don't let my smile slip until I'm back to wiping the counter.

I don't have a clue what I'm going to do. A new patron enters. His height and width have all the lads around the pool table stopping and gawking at him as he sits himself at the end of the bar. That's the thing with small towns; anyone new gets gawked at like a zoo exhibit. His eyes are downcast, and a few days' stubble coats his face. When he just waits and doesn't order, the lads go back to playing pool.

I make my way down to him with a smile. Smiling in this job is so unappreciated, but it's always important to me.

"What can I get you?" My eyes take in the bracelets on his wrist and the lace necklace that disappears under his checkered shirt.

"Carlsberg." His deep voice is what I expect. His long eyelashes lift, and he flicks me a gaze. It takes me a second to extract myself from his brown eyes.

"Coming right up," I say, more for me than him. He isn't from around here; that, I'm sure of. I would remember a face like that. I place his beer on a beer mat and take the twenty he offers me. His hands are bandaged, and some have small spots of red surfacing through.

I ring it up and return his change as Paul arrives at the counter. He eyes the stranger as he orders three beers and more coins for the pool table.

"You're not from around here?" Paul questions, but he doesn't pay Paul any attention. Instead, he picks up his pint and takes a deep drink. I'm going pretty slow at pouring the pints, but I'm interested to know where he is from.

"No," he answers, not looking at Paul.

"Where are you from?" This time, the stranger doesn't answer, and I know I need to step in. Paul's friends are also watching, and I don't want something stupid to happen. Paul, being the alpha of his group, might not like being ignored in front of his friends.

"Here are your pints," I tell Paul with a smile, getting both his attention and the attention of the stranger.

"Thanks, Ava." Paul automatically relaxes and takes the pints before returning for his change. I start to wipe down the counters, and I want to scream as Sean enters from the lounge area. Why couldn't he just stay where he was? He rattles his glass at me as he takes a seat at the opposite end of the bar.

"What can I get you, Sean?"

"Whiskey that's on you again."

I take the glass and lean into him. "I'll give you a whiskey, but it's not on me. I told you I'd get you your money." I lean out and ring up the whiskey. I don't pour it until he hands over the money, which he does.

Sean drinks the whiskey quickly while staring at me over the glass. He's had a lot to drink, and I have the right mind to cut him off, but I'll keep taking his money since he's such an asshole.

I get him another before I tidy under the counter. I know when I'm being watched, and right now, I am. I clash with a set of brown eyes. My eyes flicker to his half pint, and he follows my gaze before picking up the beer and finishing it.

I make my way down to him. "You want another?" I ask. There's something about his eyes that pulls me in but also make me want to run. It's an odd sensation.

"Yeah, thanks." He speaks with a tilt of his chin.

My eyes flicker to his bandaged knuckles before returning to him. I'm more curious than normal about this guy. I want to know what happened to his hands. Was he in a fight? What would he be like when he's angry? Right now, there's a calm about him, one that wouldn't bring violence to mind. I get his pint and return it, just as Sean howls for me again.

My hand tightens on the twenty that Brown Eyes hands to me, and I pull, but he doesn't release it. I'm surprised when I glance at him to find his intense stare focused on me.

I wait for him to speak, but he releases the money, and me, of his hold. I return to the till and wonder if I just imagined that. Sean howls again, and I've had enough. I'm so close to kicking him out when he squeals.

"Apologize now."

My stomach hollows out as my ex, Brian, grips Sean by the back of the neck. When Sean doesn't speak, he rattles him, and I take a step closer but am glad of the bar counter that separates us.

"Brian, please." It's whispered, but he doesn't hear me. He never has. He pulls Sean from the barstool, and I know everyone is watching. I want to go get Patrick, but I'm rooted to the spot.

"Apologize now, or I'll smash your face in."

Sean looks at me then, his face white and his eyes focused. He doesn't look like the same man who howled at me only a moment ago. Now, he's sober and afraid, and he should be.

"Sorry." He says it through clenched teeth before he yelps as Brian squeezes his neck tighter.

"Say it nicely," he tells Sean, and Paul and the guys giggle. Everyone is watching my landlord's humiliation. Now I'll definitely be kicked out of my apartment.

"Brian." I speak louder this time, and he finally looks at me. "He's just a drunk. It's fine." The towel I grip in my hand does nothing to relieve the stress pouring through my body.

Once again, I'm ignored as Brian leans into Sean. "You will say sorry, and in a very nice tone."

He's enjoying this too much. He always was a bully. I fell for his looks. With bright blue eyes and blond hair, he is attractive. That and muscles that seem to bulge on every part of his body just add to the appeal. And he isn't a good boy. He isn't a boy you get to keep, but I saw the challenge and tried to tame a beast. Only, the beast turned on me.

"I'm sorry, Ava," Sean says, but I take no pleasure in his humiliation.

"It's okay, Sean." I feel terrible. Brian gives him a final shake before he lets him go. My fingers unlock from the cloth, and I flex them as I watch my landlord leave. Now I wish I was going with him. Brian is smiling at me, and I try to keep the disgust from my face.

"You on a break soon?" I flicker a glance around the room. Paul and his friends are playing pool, but I can tell they aren't focused. The stranger is nursing his pint. I can't really tell if he's listening or not.

"Yeah, just let me tell Patrick," I answer. I know saying no to him would be pointless. He'd barge in and demand that Patrick let me go.

I knock on Patrick's door as he's getting up. "Ah, I was just about to come out." I force a smile.

"It's quiet and all, but I was wondering if I could take five," I ask, and he's nodding while shooing me with his hands.

Brian is out back smoking a fag. It's gotten dark, and I shiver for more than one reason. I stay close to the door just in case.

"How have you been keeping?" he asks.

It pisses me off, but I'm not dumb, so I shove that rage down, deep down.

"Yeah, fine. What do you want, Brian?" I ask. A small amount of anger slips through into my words, and he stands a bit straighter making me flinch.

His eyes widen and he looks away, brows furrowed, before returning his glance back at me. The anger in his eyes darkens them.

"Shit, Ava. I'm sorry."

I've heard this song a hundred times. Folding my arms over my chest, I look away. I don't respond, but as he approaches, I'm alert and take a step back.

"Fuck's sake, Ava. You're acting like I'm some sort of fucking animal." His voice rises, and the hairs on my neck stand.

I'm shaking my head at him, but I should be saying he isn't an animal. But he is, and I have some pride left in me. I also don't want him to hit me again.

"I need to go back in," I tell him, but I don't move. There's no point without his approval. I don't get it.

"I want you back."

My eyes burn at his words and the gentle way he looks at me now. That's what I fell in love with, a gentle giant, the side of him that rippled through my heart but wasn't real.

I shake my head as my eyes continue to well up. I want to cry in his arms and tell him how this guy, a monster, put his hands on me. I want to send Brian to beat the living shit out of him. I stand back and push down my tears.

"No," I say, and with all the courage I can muster up, I walk back into the bar. My eyes scan the empty bar and land on Patrick, but his attention is on Brian, who I know stands behind me.

I wait with stiff shoulders until Brian walks past me. His words leave a trail behind him and reach me, strangling the air from my lungs. "We'll chat again."

Like hell we will is my weak ass comeback that I don't even say out loud.

The night drags, with a few regulars coming and going. Patrick stays with me, and a few times, he tells me I can go home if I want. But I have nothing to go home to. It's midnight by the time I leave and make my way up to the Rose Garden's takeaway. There's a few cars around, but the night has really cooled. My breath puffs out as I look left and right before running across the road.

Mae's pub has a few people outside smoking. The smoking ban hurt every pub in Ireland, except the ones who don't stick to the rules after hours. Like where I work. Smyth's turns into a smoking zone when they lock the doors, and the pub doesn't officially close until the last patron leaves. It's that kind of pub.

I look behind me several times, getting the feeling that I'm being watched. But each time I peer over my shoulder, no one is there.

The heat of the Chinese is lovely, and I order a three in one before sitting on the mahogany bench. The Rose Garden is like every Chinese place around. All black shiny exterior with gold writing. On the back wall inside is a gold dragon with lots of floating lanterns around it. The door opens, and I find myself stiffening while looking up, waiting for Brian to appear, but it's not him, just some drunk guy.

The sense of being watched follows me the whole way home and doesn't stop until I close my apartment door.

CHAPTER FOUR

CONNOR

S HE ISN'T WHAT I was expecting. It's been a long time since any woman has really caught my attention. Ava—her name suits her. I had to walk away when Brian arrived into the pub. What she was doing with him was beyond me, and it didn't match the picture that had started to form in my mind until he came in and smashed it. Her emerald green eyes seemed innocent and soft; yet at times, her eyes carried so much weight, like someone who had seen too much. I can tell she's a hard worker. Her boss is fond of her, but the man who kept asking for money isn't.

Now, after seeing her with Brian, I realize I've gotten her wrong. He's a huge cocaine supplier. I've never spoken to him personally, but Shane has. He's bad news. But she's obviously his or one of his client's. Maybe that's how she got tied up in this whole mess.

I'm leaning against an abandoned bakery wall when she finally leaves the pub. It's well past midnight, and I follow her up the street. I stick to the shadows, and I watch her peek back several times. There's something vulnerable about her. There seems to be a fear in her eyes when she peers over her shoulder. I walk slower and hope it will lesson her fear.

She enters a takeaway, and now I know I should leave, but I don't. I feel responsible for scaring her; she looks pale as she keeps looking up at the Chinese door, so I feel like I should make sure she gets home safely. I wait until she gets her food, and once she closes the door to her apartment building, I walk away with an odd sense that she's safe for now.

But Brian springs back to mind. She could be up there now, snorting lots of powder up her nose. The thought disgusts me, and I want to punch something or someone.

Brian. I want to punch Brian.

My ringing phone has me turning away from her apartment and making my way back to my car that I left up near a park. It isn't a long walk, and I stuff the phone back into the pocket. It's Shane, and right now, I don't want to hear what he has to say. The roads are empty as I make my way back to Whitewood House. It was never home to me; I never felt like I was part of that place. The thoughts of going in has me hitting speed dial.

The phone only rings twice before Neill picks up. "You're alive. Where have you been?" The drum of music pulses in the background, and I know exactly where Neill is. Something in me gravitates toward it.

"Are you looking for a fighter tonight?" I ask, and I can hear him yelp to the crowd. "Connor O'Reagan is coming tonight."

I can hear the roar of the crowd. It's not that anyone likes me; they love money.

"The usual spot?" I ask, coming close to the house, but doing a u-turn on the empty road.

"Don't you fucking know it." His laughter rings through the phone, and I hang up and floor the car. It's not far away. White-wood Lake is the perfect spot at night for fighting.

A lot of headlights shine in on the makeshift ring. Tomorrow morning, when dog walkers come down here, they will never know what took place. Neill is always very careful about cleaning up after his fights. No litter, no blood stains—gravel covers the blood and litter is collected. He wants to make sure his operation never gets shut down.

I get out of the car, already feeling pumped, and music blasts from speakers in someone's boot while the crowd roars at the two men who fight. Neill is looking around him. When his eyes land on me, he jumps down from the roof of a car that he's using as his stage. He jumps onto the bonnet before he lands on the ground and disappears from sight. At four foot tall and being a punching bag his whole life, it makes you understand how resilient people can be. He made a bargain with his bullies: if they fought others instead of him, he could make them rich.

"Connor, you snake. What grass have you been lying in?"

"I think you've grown an inch," I tell him, and he shows me his runners.

"Nah, I got larger soles put in."

I grin as I remove my coat.

"Got five fights for you. Are you up for it?" he asks while shuffling on butty legs and throwing pretend punches. This is why he's such a great business man. He is always underrated. The underdog.

"Let's go." I didn't come prepared, so I strip down to my jeans, removing everything else. The cold bites at me, but once I move into the crowd, the heat makes me shiver.

The fight ends as I step into the circle. The winner is beaten and bloody; his opponent lies on the ground. Neill has his muscle clear it away quickly so I can begin.

I bounce up and down on my feet. My heart starts to race as darkness closes in. The fear that always overtakes me is here, hovering over my shoulder, and I do everything not to run. Keeping my fists clenched and my focus on the ground, I don't look up as my opponent enters the ring. His feet don't shuffle or bounce, and when I glance up, I can see the fear, and my fear eats it up. I punch quick and hard.

He hits the ground, and the crowd pulses, roars, soars so close to me. I want them to move back. I find Neill and nod. The next guy is placed in front of me, each as easy as the last. When the fifth one falls, I finally leave the ring feeling tired. It's what I need. I want to sleep tonight, and now, I think I just might.

More cars have arrived, and I pull on my clothes as Neill counts out my winnings and hands me a large stash of cash. I shove it into my pocket as a Mercedes pulls up. Spectators from the fight stop to stare at the flashy car. My brother Finn jumps out. I haven't seen him since I returned yesterday. I heard he found himself a woman. Everyone seems to have settled down.

"Thanks," I tell Neill, and then I make my way to Finn.

"Get in the car."

I want to smile. Like he could make me. But he's my favorite brother. I don't mention my car. It can stay here; I'll get it in the morning.

I nod and climb into the car. Finn doesn't wait until I'm fully in before he's pulling out and onto the main road. I buckle my belt as he floors the car; his anger is shown in how he grips the steering wheel. Finn is gentle. For him, violence is a last resort, and I hate seeing the anger that is etched into his face. I know I've caused that. I know he has good reason to hate me. Leaving him behind wasn't easy, but staying was harder.

"I'm sorry for leaving," I tell him, but he doesn't even look at me.

"It's not easy, Finn." I want to punch something again.

"It's not easy on any of us."

I snort at his stupid fucking words. When I glance at him, he's watching me.

"At least you're blood. I'm… not." I shift, hating how uncomfortable this makes me feel, but I don't want Finn to hate me.

"Don't give me that sob story. We all have the same mother." Some anger has left his words, like I had hoped it would. I knew my words would soften him.

"He hates me," I add. I don't really care, yet it's the truth.

"He hates us all."

I snort a laugh at Finn, and when I turn to him, he's grinning. "It's great to see you," I tell him, slapping his arm. "You got bigger."

"I've been taking more care of myself." This could only mean one thing.

"A woman?" I question, and he shifts in his seat, but he has a smile on his face.

"What's her name?" I ask and sit back as he starts to tell me about a girl called Siobhan. Una already filled me in, but I wanted to hear it from my brother. It's nice to hear him happy. I listen the whole way home and even as we sit in the garage.

"I want you to meet her."

I take off my belt. "Of course," I tell him, and Finn does something we don't normally do: he hugs me. It's weird for a moment before I hug my brother back. A knock on the window has us slowly separating. I meet Shane's amused face.

"You boys need a minute?" he asks as he opens Finn's door. Neither of us speak, and he rolls his eyes. "Touchy, I see. You're both wanted." He doesn't close the door, so we climb out.

"When can I meet her?" I ask Finn as we follow Shane. Shane glances at us.

"You get to meet his new prize?" Shane asks, and I clench my fists, stopping myself from punching him.

"Don't start, Shane." Finn's strength surprises me. He wasn't ever weak, but he wasn't brave either.

"Save your strength, little Finn," Shane tells him as he pushes open a set of double doors, and there the king sits.

Along with his most faithful servant by his side, Liam. Michael doesn't acknowledge me; instead, he speaks to Finn. Two years has really aged Michael, and I take in every wrinkle. He is still well groomed and well dressed, but I can see past his expensive suits. Liam is a younger version of Michael but more dangerous.

"Go find Darragh," Michael says to Finn, and I envy Finn for getting the chance to go.

Once the door closes and Shane sits down, I join them at the table. Picking at my plasters that are bloodied and in tatters keeps my anger at bay as Michael dishes out the deeds that need to be done. I flicker him a glance every now and again. Most times, he catches my gaze.

"I want a word with Connor alone." The sheep leave me alone with Michael, and I don't fear him.

"You came back," he says with a smile.

"What do you want?" I'm not in the mood for his mind games.

"I want you by your brothers' sides where you belong."

And there it is—their sides, not his. He makes me know I don't belong but reminds me that I still have to be here.

"I don't belong here, Michael." It's odd saying it out loud. It's the first time I've said this to him.

"You're right, you don't." Michael gets up and brings back a glass canister and two whiskey glasses. I accept the one he slides across to me. His words don't hurt; instead, they give me relief. Maybe I can actually leave and not feel the need to keep returning every time I'm called.

"They say there is nothing as sorrowful as a mother without her children. I say there is nothing as sorrowful as a father with a child that isn't his."

I swallow the drink and let it burn a path down my throat. "Poor you," I tell him, and he laughs before taking a sip of his drink.

"Your brothers need you, so you will be here for my sons. I wish they didn't rely on you so much. But Finn hasn't been himself, and when Finn isn't good, Darragh goes down a very slippery path."

What a bastard. I get half up and grab the bottle and pour myself another drink.

"What about Shane and Liam? Did they miss me?" I wasn't sure why I was doing this to myself, and his eyes light up.

"As much as I." I drink the full glass again before standing.

"I'm going to stay for my brothers, but this job is my last. I want out. This is a family business, and I'm not family," I tell him, and Michael stares at me. I try not to shift under the weight his stare carries.

"We will see."

I release the glass in my hand before I smash it. We won't see. I'm out this time. I can't live like this anymore. Only this time, I'll convince Finn to come with me.

Hope can be a dangerous thing, and right now, it grows inside me. Hope that one day I won't ever have to come back to this house.

"Did you miss us?" Darragh seems to materialize from the wall, a stupid-ass grin on his face. His pupils dilate. He must have taken something.

He falls into step beside me, his shoulder brushing mine. "Want to go to a party?" He's moving to music I can't hear.

"Nah, not in the mood."

"Come on, Connor. One drink." He's walking backward in front of me.

"Just at the bar." Some of his enthusiasm dwindles, but he shrugs.

"Fine, I'll take it."

"You hear about Una and Shane?" he asks as he opens two bottles of Budweiser. I take mine, and he taps his against it before taking a deep drink.

"Yeah, I saw the happy couple when I arrived," I tell him, and he's jerking and nodding.

"She was my party buddy until he fucked it all up for me, whining like a little bitch over her."

I take a drink. "You tell him that?" I ask with a smirk, knowing he didn't.

He grins. "I'm working on it."

"Brothers." Liam arrives, and I find myself sitting a little straighter. Not because I'm afraid of him, but I want to be ready for him.

"What about you, Liam? Did you get yourself a girlfriend?" I ask, and Darragh snorts a laugh. Yeah, it's funny.

"I don't see the need to attach myself to someone like that."

"You could have just said no," I tell him as I get up and arrange the pool table.

"A game?" I ask Darragh, and he's bouncing on his toes.

"Yep, yep, yep." He's hyped, and Liam tilts his head while he observes Darragh. They have a weird bromance. Something ties them together.

I set up the game and break first. I pot none and hand over the cue to Darragh. He takes it. He's high but still steady enough.

"Solids," he tells me as he leans over the table to take the next shot.

When Darragh hands me back the pool cue, I offer it to Liam. I'm not a good player. Surprise filters through me when Liam strips off his suit jacket and unbuttons the cuffs of his shirt. Darragh shakes his head at me. I ignore it and sit at the bar, enjoying my drink. Liam starts hitting balls in and doesn't stop until there's nothing left on the table.

"You take the fun out of everything," Darragh tells him, and I laugh at the perplexed look on Liam's face.

"You want to feel special?" I ask Darragh, and he gives me the middle finger.

"Come on. I'll play you." I set up the table again, and Liam takes my spot at the bar as he watches Darragh clean the table with me.

CHAPTER FIVE

AVA

"It's only me," I shout as I wriggle the key out of the door. I deeply inhale the smell of Nan's house as I close the door behind me. The yellow-tinted window lets the light stream into the warm hallway. A large rug covers most of the floor, and three plants dominate the space.

"In here, Birdy," Nan calls from the sitting room. I take the door on the left to find her sitting in her pink-covered armchair. It doesn't fit in with the rest of the room, but it's a bit like Nan—she doesn't fit in with this world. After kissing her softly on the cheek, I sit down on the cream couch that's always clean. Not a speck of dirt would get past Nan's inspection. The room is dust free. All the silverware is sparkling and displayed on her shelving.

"Sorry for not getting around sooner. Work has been crazy."

She's already waving off my explanation. "I know you youngsters do be busy Twittering and Facebooking."

I smile but don't correct her. I don't even have a smartphone. I hate technology and avoid social media at all costs.

"A cup of tea?" I ask, and she's up out of her chair. I tower over Nan. At four foot six, she's such a cute old person. That is until she opens her mouth, and you soon realize that she can take care of herself.

Her navy trousers and cream short-sleeved top sit perfectly on her small frame. Nan has the kettle on and has me sitting at the table as she moves around her small kitchen, cutting brown bread and setting the table.

"I had a visitor recently," she says as she places the tomatoes on the table.

I remove my coat and place it on the counter. "Oh, Father Gerry?" I ask, as he is a regular.

"No, that lovely young man you were dating." Nan places a plate and knife in front of me, but I'm frozen.

"Brian?" I ask while hoping she says no, but I know it's him. He was the only one I let her meet, because I thought he was *the one*.

"Yes, Brian. He came in and had a cup of tea with me."

At each word, my mouth waters and my stomach sours. I force a smile. "What did he want?" Nan is leaning against the table now, her hands pressed into the surface. Her lips are slightly puckered, and I know that face. It's one she uses when she wants me to listen to her.

"He's a nice young man, Ava. And I was very sorry to hear you had broken up with him. Broke that boys heart."

Right now, I would love to tell her that he hit me, but I don't want my nan to know that side of life. When I don't respond, she pours out the tea and places brown bread on my plate.

"You should give him a second chance," Nan adds as I mechanically sugar and milk my tea. A second chance isn't going to happen, but the thought of him visiting my nan doesn't sit right.

"I need you to promise me something," I say, and Nan nods. "If he ever calls here again, ring me, but don't let him in."

Nan's nostrils flare. "What did he do?" She's reaching for my hand, and I love her fierce protectiveness.

"Nothing. I just I don't love him, Nan, and he shouldn't be coming around here telling you his problems." God, he would hurt her too if he thought he could get to me.

I start to butter my brown bread, hoping my statement was said easily enough that she doesn't question me further.

"He's a nice boy."

"He hit me." There, I said it. And I regret it as Nan's face contorts in disbelief before it's replaced with anger.

"And to think I let that toe rag in my house." She stands, looking around the kitchen. I'm not sure what for, but I pat her hand.

"Sit down and have your tea. Just promise me that he won't be in this house again."

Nan pats my face gently. "He hurt you."

I push down the tears that burn the back of my throat. "No, I'm fine, but I don't want to see him again."

"A man puts his hands on a woman once, he'll do it again." She's shaking her head now. "He was so sweet and nice."

"Nan, I know. But promise me you won't let him in."

"I promise, Ava."

I don't feel content. "And don't you dare try to confront him." I can see it in her eyes now, and I nearly bring back up the small bit of tea I've drunk as the image of Brian hurting her comes to mind. When she doesn't reply, I say sternly, "Nan!"

"Fine, I won't. But that boy deserves a piece of my mind." Good Lord, but I need her to understand.

"That boy would hurt you. Do you hear me?"

She tuts but finally agrees not to confront him or let him in. I finish the tea at Nan's, but the moment I'm out the door, I ring Brian.

"Well, hello, beautiful."

I want to spit at my phone. "You were at my nan's," I say harshly.

"Wow, wow, calm down. I only called to see how she was."

"Don't bullshit me. We both know what you were doing."

"And what is that, Ava?" Anger is now filling his words. It doesn't take long to piss him off; I learned that the hard way. I stop walking and watch the cars zoom past as I try to think of a way out of this.

"Can we meet?" I ask with closed eyes.

"Sure. Now?"

My stomach tightens. "Yeah, now. At the café."

He agrees to meet me there in twenty. It will take me about fifteen minutes to reach it on foot. I'm not sure if what I'm doing is right or wrong, but all I know is that I can't have him near my nan ever again.

***

I arrive and grab us an empty booth near the back, hoping we can have a semiprivate conversation. I remove my coat and fidget with the menu as I wait. My blue nail polish, which is the same color as my eyes, is chipped, and I'm tempted to start picking at it, but instead, I file it away as a job to do later.

I know immediately when he arrives. It's like the air shifts. He greets nearly everyone as he makes his way to me. He must be looking into each booth, but he knows where I am. We always sat in this booth.

When he appears, he smiles. "Just like old times." That smile once captured me. He looks good today, but he always does.

I tell myself to stay on track.

He slides in across from me and unzips his red top, only to reveal a red T-shirt—my favorite color on him. Now I wonder if the color choice was intentional. He looks down and swipes a hand across it.

"For you," he tells me, and I want to slap him with the menu. But I manage a smile that doesn't trick him, as his own falls from his face.

"You wanted to meet. So talk." He's all business, and the way he looks at me tells me that I'm already so far out of my depth with him.

"My nan. She's off-limits." I say it sternly, even as he raises one blond eyebrow.

"Is that an order?" His lip tugs slightly as he speaks, as if me giving an order is funny.

"Yes. Yes, it is, Brian. I don't want her dragged into this. I won't have it." I force as much power into my words as I can, but Brian is laughing, and I watch as he throws his head back and really laughs it up.

"Oh, little Ava. You are so cute when you're serious." What an arrogant asshole. My blood boils, and I want nothing more than to get up and walk out of this place.

"Okay, don't get mad." He takes my hands, which I immediately yank out of his.

"Don't touch me." It's out of my mouth before I can think, and his eyes darken, his laughter gone.

"It was once. An accident." He's talking low, gently, and I just... can't, so I look away from him.

"I'm sorry, Ava. It won't ever happen again. Give me a second chance." *That's never going to happen.* "I promise I'll leave your nan alone if you give me a second chance."

Now I glare at him as he sits back, looking smug, and my stomach roils at the idea of ever letting him touch me again, but keeping Nan safe is my number one priority.

"Let me think about it." I hope my words sound real.

Brian tilts his head left and right before agreeing. I can't say I feel relief, because I don't, and I end up having to sit with him for another twenty agonizing minutes as he talks about himself. How could I not see what a self-centered asshole he is?

CHAPTER SIX

AVA

I LEAVE THE CAFé and walk another ten minutes to Super Value. I need to buy some food. Shopping hasn't been on the top of my agenda lately, but since Nan mentioned how thin I've gotten, I decided that I needed to get some proper food in and stop eating takeaways.

It's a Thursday, so there aren't many around in the grocery store. I grab a basket and start off in the fruit and veggie section. I get a few bananas and some spuds and turnips. I'm browsing in the bread aisle, looking for non-white, maybe something nutty, when a large frame moves further down the aisle. He reminds me of the stranger from the other night in the bar.

He doesn't turn around, so I take my time watching him and then focus on the bread for a moment. I don't want to look like a stalker. His jeans fit him snuggly, and he's even larger now that I see him standing. He must be six foot or more. His wide shoulders covered in a green-and-navy checked shirt. The sleeves of his shirt are rolled up, and different-colored bands are around his wrist. Large hands pick up a package of Swiss Rolls, strawberry flavored. I grab bread and put it into my basket as I take a step closer to him. He's still looking in the dessert aisle, and maybe I could do with a pack of cookies. I move even closer, and his cologne causes my stomach to squeeze. It's a really rich and musky smell.

I'm close enough that if I reached out, I could touch him. I pick up a pack of Jammie Dodgers and put them into my basket. I've lingered too long and decide to move along, but not without one final glance.

He's watching me from under thick lashes. Lines mar his forehead like he's confused, and it's sexy as hell.

"Hi," I say, and his nostrils flare ever so slightly.

"Ava. Hi." Him knowing my name is like a quick electrical shot to my body. Hearing him say it in his deep voice is more than nice. I don't ask how he knows it, as he must have heard the guys call to me a thousand times in the pub.

He holds out his free hand to me, and I stare at it like it's a foreign object. "Connor," he tells me, and I take his warm hand that still has bandages around the knuckles.

"Nice to meet you, Connor." I'm smiling now. He's a good head taller than me and peering up into his brown eyes could really tangle up a girl.

"Didn't take you for a Jammie Dodger kind of girl."

It takes me a moment to gather my hormones as he smiles, flashing a set of straight white teeth. My laugh is a little too high, and I try to settle down. "Didn't take you for a strawberry Swiss Roll kind of guy," I say, and this time, he looks confused until he glances at his basket.

"I didn't put that in here. It must have fallen in," he says as he places it back on the shelf, and I laugh.

"No, I'm pretty sure you put the Swiss Rolls in there."

He shakes his head, keeping a pretty straight face. "Are you sure?"

I shift my basket from one arm to the other. "Yes. I saw you."

"So you were watching me."

My stomach erupts with butterflies as he dips his head, looking at me once again from under his lashes.

"No... Yes."

He's laughing, and it's like freshly melted chocolate. So good. He puts the Swiss Roll back into his basket, and I can't keep the stupid grin from my face.

"Maybe we could grab a coffee." He says it so offhandedly, but I'm nodding before I can form words.

"I finish work around ten tonight if you want to get one then." I have it said before I realize it sounds silly.

"Sounds great, Ava." My name on his lips again sends my stomach somersaulting.

"Okay, I'll meet you outside my work place, then. At ten," I say, just to clarify as I shift my basket again.

"See you at ten."

I'm smiling, he's smiling. I can't believe I have a date and one that was set up in the dessert aisle of a supermarket.

"Bye," I say to his retreating form, and he smiles over his shoulder and gives me a curt nod. Once he's out of sight, I have the urge to do a little clap, but I don't. Instead, I look around me and wonder if anyone was listening to our conversation.

I only live, like, ten minutes away, but the walk with two heavy bags of groceries is killing me. The only thing keeping me smiling is thinking of Connor. His name suits him. I like it. I have to put the bags on the ground as I get my key out of my pocket. I open the door and reach for my bag, but I want to walk right back out. My landlord is standing in the hall, talking to the owner of the bookies.

They both turn to me as I close the door behind me. The bookie owner—I can't think of his name—has snow-white teeth against an artificial tan. His hair is dyed jet black. The overall appearance is stark. His pink jumper and shirt just make him look ridiculous. I look at Sean as he says goodbye to the bookie. His brown trousers and brown jumper suit his shitty personality. He turns to me with a face, and I try to get around him to go up the stairs to my apartment, but he won't move.

"I don't have your money today," I tell him. I don't tell him that I haven't been paid from work. But he's nodding.

"I don't want your money. I want you out. This is your two weeks' notice." He moves aside to let me go up the stairs, and I climb the steps with my head held high. I wasn't going to argue, but I wasn't sure what I was going to do.

***

For a Thursday night, it's busy. Paul and his friends are back in, taking up the pool table, and a few locals and some students make up the rest. I'm the only one on. Patrick is in the office, so if I need him, he isn't far away. I leave to collect glasses. Arriving back to put them in the washer, I see I have a new customer settling in at the bar.

"A Carlsberg?" I ask as I make my way toward Connor. He looks good in a white polo shirt, the top few buttons opened, letting me see smooth tanned skin.

"A 7UP would be great."

I raise both eyebrows with a smile, and he tilts his head and smiles, making my heart race.

"I have a coffee date tonight. Don't want to be drinking."

I'm smiling from ear to ear as I get him his 7UP. "Who's the lucky girl?" I tease, placing a beer mat in front of him before putting the glass on it.

"She's a barmaid. Really pretty."

His words are making my stomach twist. I wipe down the counter near him before I flicker him a gaze. "I hope you have fun," I tell him, and he nods, his smile gone as he glances at someone in the mirror behind me. My smile goes too as I look up, only to have Harry the absolute asshole in front of me. I'm surrounded by a lot of assholes in my life.

"Ava, have you seen this man?" I don't look at the picture he's holding up.

"No," I answer Harry and try to walk away.

"Ava, look at the picture." Harry has the decency to add please when I stare at him. His small blue eyes shift back and forth; he can't keep eye contact.

"Now you decide to do your job?" I bark, knowing I'm being foolish. Harry leans in, stubble coating his face, making him look dishevelled. Some men look sexy with stubble, but he just looks like he needs a wash.

"Have you something to say?" I can hear the undercurrent of a threat, so I give the picture about a two-second glance, and my stomach curls. I've seen this man, but he wasn't in the best condition. At the time, I thought he was dead until Brian said he was really wasted, and Brian and another guy carried him out of the pub.

"Why, what happened to him?" I ask, and Harry waves the photo.

"Have you seen him?"

"No," I say, lying to a Gardaí for the first time in my life, but Harry shouldn't be allowed on the force. He can be bought by anyone who will give him money.

"Lying to the Gardaí is an offense."

I want to roll my eyes at him, but he just might arrest me to spite me. "It's a good thing I'm not a liar," I tell him and walk away to serve a customer. This time, he doesn't stop me.

It settles down, and Patrick arrives out of the back, letting me finish my shift. I grab my bag and coat, but when I look up, Connor is gone.

My heart deflates, and I find myself standing, staring at his stool longer than what's normal.

"You okay?" It's Patrick's voice that shakes me out of my slumber, and I nod, force a smile, and decide to just head home. Well, what will be home for the next two weeks.

I'm smiling because as I step outside, I see Connor leaning against the wall of an abandoned building across the road. He gives me a salute, and his lip tugs up on the left as he jogs across the road.

"Are you ready for the coffee?" he asks, and I nod while I start walking. Glancing at him, I see he's following.

"You like what you do?" His question is one I have the answer to but hate saying because I like Patrick so much. Stuffing my hands into my pockets keeps them warm against the cold.

Connor has done the same. A heavy navy coat hides that fabulous white polo shirt and smooth skin.

"Not really, no. But it pays the bills, sort of." Now I'm mumbling. It would pay the bills, but I have too many bills.

"Sort of?" Connor questions, and I fire a quick glance at him sideways. He's watching me.

"Yeah, it's nothing. Just in a hobble. But I'll get out of it. I always do." I smile at him now, and he nods, but he doesn't look convinced.

We arrive at the café that I had only met Brian, what was it, a few hours ago? But it was the best in town and stayed open until late.

"Will we sit outside?" I ask, wanting to stay in the cool air. For me, being in a warm place and having to talk about myself made me uncomfortable. But outside, I felt like I could breathe and talk. I'm not entirely sure why, but it worked better for me.

"Perfect. What will I get you?"

I decide then, as I sit down, that Connor is definitely over six foot.

"How tall are you?" My question causes a smirk to grow on his face.

"Six foot four. How tall are you?"

"Five foot six. And I'll have a latte."

Connor nods, still wearing the smirk, and leaves to get our coffees.

I inhale the fresh air while pulling my sleeves down over my fingers. There's a bite in the night air, but I love how fresh it is. The small roads are now empty, and a few people stroll down the streets. Street lamps give a nice orange hue down on the cobbled pavements.

I keep shifting in my seat while glancing at the door. The door and windows are covered in frosted glass, so I can't see in. I cross my legs just as Connor arrives with two lattes and one Danish.

Taking my latte from him, I watch as he bends his large frame into the chair. Being this close to him has my stomach fluttering as his aftershave assaults me.

"Have you lived here long?" This is the part of getting to know each other I hate. So I sip my latte as Connor rips the Danish in half. I take the half he offers me and tear off a small piece.

"No. I moved to Kells a month ago, but my landlord just gave me two weeks' notice, so I'm not sure where to next." I bite my lip, surprised at the emotion the words evoke in me. "What about you?" I ask and sip my latte, which is so divine and frothy.

"Whitewood area. I wouldn't call it home, but it's where I live."

"I know that area. It's nice," I say. My eyes once again get drawn to his hands, still bandaged. When I look back up, he's watching me.

"You should just ask. I've seen you look at my hands a lot."

I bite my lip again, hating how transparent I am. "Okay, what happened to your hands?" I shrug like it's no big deal, and his lip tugs slightly before it settles down.

"I fight for money."

Both my eyebrows rise. I wasn't exactly expecting that. "Like Conor McGregor?"

His laugh is deep and husky, and I drink it up. "No, not like Conor McGregor."

I nod like I know what he's talking about, but I don't. "So, illegal?" I spit out and want to kick myself as lines appear on his forehead. "Sorry, never mind," I say quickly.

He sits back. "No, it's illegal. But I'm in between jobs, and right now, it's cash."

"Anything in mind you'd like to do?" I ask him, studying his full lips. They are moist from the latte.

"I want to open my own shop."

That surprises me. He doesn't look like the entrepreneur type; more like the construction type. "What kind of shop?"

I pick at my Danish, and for the first time since we sat down, he looks uncomfortable and moves in his seat. His thumb rubs his upper lip.

"Like art." He's frowning again, the sexy lines distracting me. "I make wooden ornaments." His frown deepens, and I want to tell him to cut it out. I can't even function.

"What about you? What would you like to do?"

I'm back in the spotlight, the awkwardness between us gone. I want to ask more about the wooden ornaments, but I can see we've moved past that.

"Honestly, I don't know. College isn't for me. I don't have any real skills, though I like working with people."

"Yeah, I see that in the bar. You're good with people." His compliment is really nice, and I smile.

"But you didn't seem to like the guard. An ex?"

I nearly spit out my latte at his question. "Harry?" I ask while shaking my head, and I can see that Connor is fighting to hide a smile. "No, no. He's just an asshole."

A small laugh bubbles from his lips, and I'm transfixed.

"Why is he an asshole?" Connor asks before drinking deeply from his latte. I don't know if it's how he asks or the topic, but it's like he's trying to sound casual—but the question isn't. My thought process makes no sense to me.

"Ah, it's stupid history. Not worth talking about."

My answer has him nodding slowly. "I just thought it was deeper between you two."

I shift in my seat, my moral compass kicking in. Maybe lying wasn't the brightest idea. I want to change the subject. This is all making me uncomfortable.

Picking up my latte, I answer him. "Nope, just silly stuff. So tell me about these wooden ornaments." Now he looks awkward, and I know it was a bit of a soft spot. But I really want to know.

Connor takes in a deep breath before leaning both arms on the table. "I carve people from wood." He doesn't look gentle enough to do something like that. But I take his word for it. We talk for a while longer until the café closes. It's near midnight before Connor walks me to my apartment door.

I had a lovely time," I say while stuffing my hands into my pockets. His eyes have shot to my lips several times since we stopped, and I wonder if he is going to kiss me.

"Maybe we can do this again," he says, jutting out his chin, and I smile.

"I'd love that." My words have his lips tugging up.

He takes a step backward. "Good night, Ava," he tells me, and I'm struggling with admiring him for leaving it at that and cursing him for not kissing me.

"Good night, Connor," I tell him as I duck in the door. I smile as I take the steps two at a time. But it dissolves as Brian leans against my door.

CHAPTER SEVEN

CONNOR

I ARRIVE BACK AT Whitewood House near one in the morning. Voices from the main foyer have me pausing.

"She was still alive." It's Finn's, and it's the strain in his voice that has me pushing the door open. The whole family is there.

Darragh and Finn sit on the couch closest to the door, the arch allowing me to see more of Finn than Darragh, while Shane stands near an unlit fireplace. Liam and their father sit on two Queen Anne chairs.

Shane glances at me with raised eyebrows. "Where's your phone?"

Shit. I had turned it on silent when I was with Ava. "I was on a job," I say as I take it out of my pocket and light up the screen to see seven missed calls.

"What's happened?" I ask, and Finn looks from me to Shane, worry etched on his face.

"Nothing. We just all need to stay calm and not get so excited." Liam speaks to where Finn and Darragh are sitting, and I sit down on the couch opposite the fireplace.

"Excited about what?" I ask Liam directly. His suit jacket is open. He sits nearly half off the Queen, his waist coat buttoned, and everything sitting perfectly on him.

"There seems to be a woman missing in the nearby area." His slow words are annoying me, and I'm glad when Finn speaks.

"It's Siobhan's auntie. She's missing." Finn scratches his eyebrow, his gaze flickering to Darragh, who's looking at his hand.

His subdued stare tells me something isn't right here. Darragh is always alert and loud, but now he looks unsettled.

"We should tell Connor," Shane says, looking at their father, who is observing me. I keep his stare. He glances away as Shane calls to him. "Father, Connor is family."

I snort a humorless laugh. I wasn't ever sure if all my half brothers could see the distaste that he held for me. This is the first time anyone has ever spoken out for me, and I'm shocked that it's Shane. If I had placed a bet, it would have been on Finn.

"Darragh was attacked and defended himself. In the process, the woman died."

I don't believe a word Liam says. He's really painting a sweet picture, but Darragh has always been his favorite brother. I know he's full of shit as Finn snorts.

"The woman was alive. He broke her fucking neck." Finn's anger surprises me.

My gaze flicks to Darragh, who still stares at his hands, not defending himself. "So the missing woman is dead, and what, the guards have been asking around?" I ask Liam as Michael has decided that the empty fireplace holds his attention better than me.

"They've been here asking questions, but there's nothing for anyone to worry about. We all know where we were the night it happened. Isn't that right, Darragh?" Shane's words rise, and Darragh's head snaps up. He's nodding, and his knee jerks.

"I want a word with Darragh. The rest of you leave." The king speaks, so everyone leaves one by one.

I make sure I'm the last, and he stares at me with all the hate in the world. I get up and leave slowly, not sure what my point is. Maybe to let him know he's not my king.

"You want a drink?"

I smirk at Finn. "Yeah, it would be a start," I tell him. The tension in this house is strangling me.

We go to the bar, and I sit as Finn goes behind the counter and gets a bottle of whiskey and two glasses.

"So, you want to tell me in English what's going on?" I ask, and he's shaking his head.

"It's a mess." Finn sits down and pours out two glasses of whiskey. We lightly touch our glasses and take a deep drink before Finn tells me exactly what happened, and yeah, that does sound like a mess.

"I want you to meet Siobhan this weekend." Finn looks nervous, and it makes me smile.

"Yeah, I'd like that." I squeeze his arm, and he nods. Right now, I know when I leave the next time, I'm not coming back. But leaving him doesn't feel right. I'm glad when Shane asks Finn to give us a moment. It stops the guilt that's swirling around me.

Shane takes the seat Finn vacates. I pour myself another drink. Shane declines when I tilt the bottle toward the empty glass Finn left behind. I wonder if he declined because it's Finn's glass, or if he just doesn't want a drink.

"What did she see?" Shane questions. He doesn't even blink as he waits for me to respond. I take a deep drink before answering.

"Nothing."

Shane's shaking his head, cutting me off from finishing.

"She's lying. I know she saw me." His words are low. He isn't looking at me now, his eyes focused over my shoulder like he's remembering.

"Well, if she did, she isn't saying," I answer while refilling my glass. I have no idea what's going through his head, and that worries me.

"But she will eventually." Shane rises, ready to stand, and I can't let him go. I can't leave Ava in his hands.

"You're wrong." Both eyebrow's raise, and he sits back down.

"The Gardaí arrived into the pub she was working in, and she wouldn't give them any information. They showed a picture of the guy, and she said she never saw him."

"I know she saw me." He's not convinced that she won't say. Yet he's convinced that she saw him.

"Why didn't you have her taken care of straight away?" Saying it out loud feels wrong, like a betrayal to Ava, but I need to know what is driving Shane to make a certain decision.

"I couldn't. Hurting her isn't an option. Until it's an option."

Clear as fucking glass. I let out an irritated breath, and a slow grin grows on Shane's face.

"Don't tell me you care for her." He laughs, and I release the glass in my hand before I smash it.

"I just don't understand what the big secret is." I get up even as my body wants me to sit here and find out what Shane is up to. "But yeah, she's your problem now," I add.

I stop at the door as he speaks.

"Brian is a big client of ours. He's asked for her not to be touched. So unless he says we can, or I risk going to prison, she will be left alone for now. But I want you to still keep an eye on her." I glance at Shane from over my shoulder, his words giving me mixed emotions. Now I want to know why the hell she's under his protection and what happens the moment that protection is lifted.

CHAPTER EIGHT

AVA

I T DOESN'T SEEM TO matter how much makeup I dab on my cheek, the lump and bruising is still visible. I close my eyes, not wanting to look at the girl in the mirror. How did it come to this? How did I end up being hit by a man? If I ever heard of someone hitting a woman, I honestly couldn't understand how it happened the second time. I always thought I'd be out of there and have him in court. Yet, here I am, covering up the marks that Brian left on me again.

He was angrier this time, after seeing me with Connor, and I knew he was going to hurt me. Tears fall silently down my face. I'm disgusted with myself for allowing this to happen. I want to hurt him.

My phone bleeps. I forgot I was holding it. I've rung the Gardaí station several times, only to hang up. No one will listen anyway.

I think of Connor and his admission of being a fighter. I smile as I picture him kicking the shit out of Brian. But he doesn't even know me, so Connor would have no real reason to fight him. Unless I pay him. But I have no money.

I'm thinking crazy. I check my messages to see Connor has sent me one. **I had a lovely time. Hope we can meet again soon.**

My eyes blur with unshed tears at his words.

Are you free? I type out and then erase the message. I don't know what I want—him here, him not here; for him to see me like this or not to see me like this.

I could do with some company. Only if you're free. I hit send before I can change my mind.

My eyes burn again as I realize how lonely I feel. I want my nan so bad, but I don't want to take this to her door. I need to handle this. I return to the mirror, only to see the small cut has opened again, and blood has started to seep out. Wiping off the makeup hurts like hell as I dab at the blood. It isn't deep. Brian wears rings. It's what must have cut me.

I'm back to looking at myself in the mirror, wondering how the hell I got here. Not just with Brian, but being homeless and in a shitty job with nothing to look forward to.

My phone rings, making me jump, and my heart pounds. But I answer it.

"Are you okay?" Connor's voice has me choking down the tears.

"Are you driving while on the phone?" I ask instead, and his short laugh makes me smile, but I hiss in pain.

"No, it's hands free. Are you okay?" he repeats. I can almost picture him frowning.

"Yeah, it's nothing. I hope I didn't disturb you."

"No. I'll be there in a few minutes."

My stomach jumps at that. What am I doing?

"Okay, see you then." I hang up and return to the mirror, not sure if I should try to cover it up, but touching it has it bleeding again. I let my hair fall down my back, pulling it around my face. It shadows the mark, but he'll still see it, and a part of me wants him to. A huge part.

***

The doorbell chimes, and suddenly I question what I'm wearing. I showered after Brian had left and put on gray tracksuit bottoms and a green tank top. I could have tidied up a bit more, though.

Opening the door, my heart rate spikes as Connor stands there. It's so odd to see him at my place.

"Come in." I step out of his way, but he doesn't move, and his stance is almost unnatural. Like someone has hit pause. I notice his fist clench.

"Who did this?" he asks, his eyes flickering from my face to my eyes.

"Will you come in?" I'm not going to discuss this in a hallway. You never knew who's listening. He gives a curt nod and enters.

I sit on the couch and am surprised when he sits beside me and removes his black jacket. A plain clean gray T-shirt fits him snuggly. He doesn't ask any questions, and I try not to flinch when his fingers gently examine my face.

"It's not broken, and the cut's not deep. Where's your freezer?" he asks, getting up, and I point to it.

My throat burns. I don't want to cry, so I sit and try to push the emotions that are clawing up my throat back down. Connor sits beside me and puts a frozen bag of peas to the bruise, once again with such gentleness.

"You want to tell me what happened?" Connor asks, but now I can't meet his eye.

"Just an ex," I say, trying to stop the tremble that enters my hand. It's like the shock is wearing off again. This isn't happening to someone else. It's happening to me.

Connor's silence has me peeking up at him. His clenched jaw and unblinking eyes are unsettling.

"His name."

And there it is—my chance. But I can see the violence in Connor's eyes, and I know this fight would leave him worse off. You don't hit Brian and get away with it. "I don't want to, Connor."

He removes the peas from my face and takes a look. "The swelling is going down," he tells me.

"He's hit me before." I focus on my nails. "The first time was such a shock. I loved him." Now I gather my courage and stare up at Connor. He's just as still as when I opened the door to him. I want to check that he's breathing. He blinks.

"I'm not one of those girls who stays when someone hits them." I hold my head up as I speak. "I walked away." My anger comes out in falling tears. "I left. I moved." I close my eyes to stop the onslaught of not just anger but pain now.

Heat scorches my cheeks and neck. He must think I'm crazy. Dragging him here, crying about my problems. I want to apologize before he runs out the door.

"My stepfather hit my mother," he says. My eyes snap to his. He lifts the peas again, checks my face before turning them and placing them back on my face. "My mother was such a kind and gentle woman. He was an animal to put his hands on her." The tightness around his eyes has him glaring over my shoulder.

"I didn't know at the time. I would have killed him." Connor is looking at me again, and there's something in his voice that makes me believe he really would have killed his stepfather.

"Did your mother get away?" I ask, but I can see that distant look in his eyes.

"No." His one word is monotone, and it squeezes my heart.

"I'm so sorry, Connor." I touch his free hand, and he removes the bag of peas from my face while staring down at my hand. I squeeze his large fingers, and his brown eyes snap up to mine.

"I just wish she had told me. I would have protected her." His brows furrow, and he stands, removing his hand from mine. He's a big guy when he stands, so I don't try to approach him again. There's a darkness in Connor that I want to shine a light on.

The noise of him putting the peas back in the freezer has me relaxing. I thought he might be leaving, and I don't want him to go.

"You need to ring the guards." Connor sits back down while throwing his arm along the back of the couch. I let my hair fall more around my face.

"I can't," I tell him, and the tightness around his eyes has me explaining.

"I went before to complain, and they wouldn't listen to me. Brian has some guards paid off."

"Brian." He repeats his name with flared nostrils. "The blond-haired guy."

I'm taking his hand again, and he holds it still. He doesn't wrap his fingers around mine, but he doesn't pull his hand away either. "He's really dangerous, Connor."

"So am I." Connor might be a fighter, but he's a good guy. Brian came from bad stuff—parents who were into drugs. I suppose I saw a lost boy in him when I first met him. But he's rotten to the core, just like them. But Connor has no idea, and I'm not getting him caught up in the madness of the world that I found myself in.

"Not like him, Connor. Please just leave it," I tell him, and he stares at me without blinking. It's unsettling, but it also sets my stomach erupting with butterflies.

"Move back with your nan. It will be safer." I'm shaking my head again, hating it. I'm still holding his hand, but he isn't holding mine.

"I left to protect her, Connor. She raised me, and I've lived with her my whole life, but when I discovered who Brian really was, I knew I had to leave." I release his hand and stand now. Thinking of Brian hurting her is sending my heart pounding. I don't know what to do. My throat burns again. Leaving her alone isn't an option anymore.

"Where are your parents?" I don't look at Connor as he speaks from the couch. But his voice is controlled. I can feel the tremble enter my bottom lip.

"They live a few towns over with the rest of their kids." A stray tear falls, and I wipe it away quickly. It still hurts, no matter how many times I say it.

At just a few months old, they left me behind to travel, and along the way, they forgot to come back for me. Well, it isn't that simple. I was settled and happy with Nan, so they left me with her. They stopped visiting after I was five, or so Nan told me. I don't remember them.

Large hands rest on my shoulders, and I close my eyes at the contact. His hands are so warm on my bare skin, and I fight off the shiver that moves down my arms. I want to turn, but I don't.

"I'm sorry for dragging you into my drama." I swallow my emotions and clear my throat before turning around. His hands slip from my shoulders, and he towers over me. Lines appear on his forehead as his eyes search my face.

"We have a lot in common," he says. It's whispered, and I'm not sure if he intended to say it out loud.

"Your family left you behind too?" I ask.

"Pretty much, yeah." He doesn't sound pained, and I can't look away from him. I want to know more.

When his tongue flicks out and he wets his lips, I bite my own. His eyes snap to the movement, and he exhales quickly. Large hands slowly return to my shoulders, and I step into him, brushing my lips against him. When I pull away from him, the burn of my cheek after rubbing his beard has me hissing.

"You okay?" he asks while moving back in. This time, he places his lips gently on mine, tilting his head to my unmarked cheek. His kiss is nice; it's warm. His grip leave my shoulders and finds my waist. I'm airborne. My legs wrap around him, and I feel all of him against me. His tongue enters my mouth, and I gasp, pulling him closer to me. My breasts brush against my top, and wetness pools between my legs.

Vibrations attack my hip, and it's not until Connor pulls away and the vibrations continue that I realize it's coming from his pocket. He slowly lets me down with an apologetic shrug before taking his phone out of his pocket. I watch him as he checks the screen to see who's calling. Lines appear on his forehead. He answers it.

"I'm kind of..." He steps away from me and nods. "Okay, give me twenty minutes." He finishes the call and looks at me. "A friend's house was broken into."

I fix my top and try to act as composed as he seems. "Oh my God. Is he okay?"

"I'm not sure," he answers honestly and stuffs the phone into his pocket. Rubbing his forehead with one finger, he fixes me with another apologetic shrug.

"Why don't you come with me?"

"No, I need an early night."

He nods at my answer while fishing out his keys. "When I leave, don't answer the door to anyone," he tells me.

"I won't." I never do. Brian was waiting for me. I wrap my arms around my waist.

"I feel bad leaving you." He's hunched toward me. I can see the conflict in how tense his shoulders are. I unwrap my arms.

"Don't. Thanks so much for coming. But I'm fine now, just tired." The exhaustion isn't a lie. My body feels boneless.

"Okay, if you need me for anything or if he returns, ring me."

"Of course I will," I lie easily. His fingers touch my chin, the contact warm, and I lean into him. His lips brush mine. My body seems to gravitate to him. But the kiss ends sooner than I want it to.

"I'll be in touch."

Closing the door behind Connor leaves me with mixed emotions. My fingers flutter to my lips. He can kiss. I'm smiling as I double-check the locks, but that falters as I remember why I'm doing so. The reminder seems to ignite the pain in my cheek.

CHAPTER NINE

CONNOR

WHEN I ARRIVE AT Neill's house, I don't even have to reach the front door to see the place has been trashed. Every window is smashed. The door swings open with a touch of my foot. I try to look around the door.

"Connor, is that you?"

"You alone?" I shout back before entering.

"Yeah, in the kitchen."

I move past the torn-up hall. Pictures crunch under my boots as I push open the kitchen door. Something heavy is behind it.

"Jesus, take it easy."

I duck my head around to see Neill sitting against the door. He's holding his right hand, each finger bent back at odd angles. Blood coats his white hoodie and still runs from his nose.

I squeeze through the door; a towel on the counter is my next move. I hand it to Neill, and he has to release his broken fingers.

"Who did this?" I ask him, kneeling down. Someone took a baseball bat to his kitchen. Everything is torn from the cabinets and smashed on the ground. It seemed personal.

"I don't know. There was a group of them." His nose starts to bleed again, and I push the towel back closer to him.

"You need a doctor." He's shaking his head like a broken nose and fingers will mend themselves.

"Say someone jumped you, which is pretty much the truth." I help him up.

"I can't leave the house like this." He's glancing around him.

"I don't think there's anything left to take. I'll ring a mate to come board it up."

I get him to the hospital quickly, but I don't go inside with him. Instead, I make a call to Russell, a friend who takes care of rental properties around the area. I give him Neill's address, and he promises to do it soon.

I ring Ava, only to get her voice mail. She said she was tired; maybe she's sleeping. I send her a quick message in case she is awake. I wait a few moments but don't get a response. The hospital is quiet, and I find Neill easily. He's loud and has the nurses laughing.

"Here is my friend I was telling you about." The nurses turn to me, and I wonder what he's been saying about me.

"Very brave of you to scare off seven men," one of them says, and I look to Neill, but he shrugs.

"Seven? By the time we leave, it might be ten," I say and get a quick laugh before they leave. Neill has a plaster across his face, and his fingers are in bandages too.

"All broke?" I ask, and he nods.

"Did they say anything?"

"The nurses?" he questions, and I fold my arms across my chest.

"Neill, the guys who smashed up your house."

He glances away, and I know he's withholding.

"Look, it's no skin off my nose. But if you want help, you know I'm here."

"I knew the guys. They lost money at a fight and didn't like it."

"Why wouldn't you just say that?" I ask, leaning against the wall.

"Because it makes me look weak. Word gets out, everyone will be smashing up my house because they didn't win. I may as well quit."

"Retaliate," I tell him, and he hops off the bed.

"How, Connor?" He waves his injured arm in the air and pulls it back.

"Fuck." I glance around, seeing we've attracted the attention of an elderly couple. I apologize to them, but they look away.

"Me. I'll retaliate," I tell him, and he stops petting himself and glances up at me, a slow grin tugging at his lips.

"You'd do that?"

"Why not?" I tell him. I leave before he starts hugging me. I'm in the hall only a few moments when my phone dings with a message from Ava.

In bed. How's your friend? Oh and thanks so much for tonight. X

I smile before firing back a text. **He's fine, nothing serious.** I glance up from the phone as Neill, looking anything but fine, walks toward me.

"You ready to go?"

"Yep, just have a load of pain meds." He yaps on as we head to the car. I finish typing the text. **My pleasure, if you need me just ring. x**

I stuff the phone into my pocket as we climb into my car.

"Have you a place to stay?" I ask. I don't want to bring him back to mine, but if he has nowhere else, I will. He tells me he's staying with his mother, who lives in the next estate. I drop him off.

"Send me the names and address of the guys," I tell him, and he nods.

"I don't have them all, but I'll get them."

I smirk. I know he will.

There aren't any lights on when I arrive at Whitewood House, but that doesn't mean no one's awake. Someone is always hanging around. I enter my room downstairs. It's always been my room. Everyone else stayed upstairs except for Liam, who took over the basement area.

My phone vibrates, and I pull it out of my jeans pocket as I strip off my jacket.

A word in the library.

I could ignore Liam's message, but I don't. He must have heard me arrive. He's sitting on one of the Queen Anne's. It's a rare thing, but he looks thoughtful. His brows are furrowed, two fingers touching his chin thoughtfully.

"You called," I say, and he doesn't startle. He looks up and beckons me to come over with two fingers. So very fucking Michael.

"I'm tired," I tell him.

"It won't take long," is his response. "I'll be blunt. Why did you cross into the north?"

My heart thumps heavily. I blink, knowing I should have some outward reaction. I'm too still, so I lean back into the chair.

"When?" I fire back, and he nods as if to say two can play this game.

"Father's informant was tailing you."

This information doesn't surprise me. But coming from Liam, it does. "Michael knew of my whereabouts at all times?" I clench my jaw. Why wait two years, then? To see what I was doing? If he knew, I would be dead by now.

"I was in Monaghan for work. That's as far into the north as I went. I'm tired, Liam." I rise, and Liam doesn't speak until I'm at the door.

"So you never crossed into Belfast?"

I'm glad my back is to him. "Michael's informant is mistaken," I say.

"I don't really care what you were doing in Belfast. Just don't bring anything to our door."

I stare at him. "This house is filled with secrets already, Liam," I fire back. "What could I possibly do?"

"It's not a secret if it's known by three people."

I reenter the room against my better judgment. Resting a hand on either side of Liam's head, I lean into him.

"I'm not afraid of you," he says. "And I'm not fucking stupid either. Say what you want to say." His unemotional response makes me want to plummet his face in, but I use my better judgment and lean out.

"It is a secret if the three people are you, Shane, and Michael." Because those are the three people in the house that have the darkest secrets.

"You're hiding something," he says calmly, and I smile. He must hate not having a clue, and if he's asking, then he doesn't know.

I am hiding something. I'm here to find out which one of these fuckers killed my mother. I'm not sure which one, but I will find out.

"Good night, Liam," I call over my shoulder.

***

It's four in the morning when my phone wakes me. I'm lying over my blankets, fully clothed. I'm used to sleeping like this in case I have to run and move. Realizing that Michael knew where I was the whole time made every uncomfortable night's sleep for nothing.

I rub my face before looking at the message on my phone. It's from Neill. It's the list I've been waiting for—the names and addresses of five men. I pull on my boots and jacket, knowing this is the release I need.

I'm standing in Darragh's room, not really expecting him to be there, but he is. He's wearing last night's clothes and is strewn across his double bed. The smell of alcohol has me thinking that maybe I should go it alone.

His floor is coated with clothes. Every drawer in his dresser is pulled open; wardrobe doors sit wide open as well. His room is a mess. It's four times the size of mine, but I wouldn't want this luxury. I would feel like I owed Michael something.

"Wake up." I kick his leg. Blue eyes flicker open as he glances up at me, squints, and closes his eyes.

"That really you, Connor?" he asks the gray-striped quilt.

"I need to go hurt some people. You in?"

He's up, and I'm grinning at his eagerness. He grabs a pair of beige boots and notices he already has runners on. Dropping them on the floor, he pats down his white shirt and suit jacket.

"Good to go," he tells me, slapping his face a few times.

It's four thirty in the morning when I reach the first house. They all live in Kells, but I'll do them one night at a time to build up their fear and panic, wondering when they will be next. The first house on the list is a small bungalow. It will be easy to break in to. The garden out front is neatly trimmed, but there isn't a flower or pot in sight. I hope this is a sign that David lives alone. I hate when women or kids are around. They overcomplicate things.

The balaclava I tug over my face feels heavy, but the feeling will settle. I glance at Darragh, and he does the same. We've done this before, and Darragh's presence adds excitement to the job.

Bat in hand, I climb out of the car and creep along the sidewalk. Streetlights cast pockets of light as we move slowly toward our target. Darragh follows suit. His bat has blue eyes with long lashes and large red lips painted on the top of it. He named the bat Rochelle, and now he strokes it.

We reach the back door easily. The back garden is a mirror version of the front. I'm kneeling down, screwdriver in hand as I pop the lock. The door opens easily, and a small dog stares at me.

Fuck.

"Kill it," Darragh whispers behind me.

"I'm not killing a dog," I whisper back while rising and sliding the screwdriver into my pocket. The dog's tail wags, and I'm just glad he isn't barking. I wonder how much time we have left before he starts. It could be seconds. I hold my hands out toward the dog.

"I'll kill it." Darragh moves in front of me, and I sidestep to let him pass. Entering the small kitchen with its green eighties style cabinets and fittings, I turn to Darragh.

"Here, doggy," he says softly, and the dog backs away from him, movings toward the hall door that sits open.

"Don't kill it, Darragh," I warn him. He grabs the dog quickly, its bark lodging in its throat as Darragh holds it by the snout.

"Darragh," I warn, and he tilts his head. I can see the laughter in his eyes, so I pass him and the dog and walk into the hall. No lights are on, and I push open the sitting room door carefully. The room is empty. A small two-seater couch and TV take up most of the area.

The space is smaller than the kitchen. I move back into the hall and flicker a gaze up the stairs. A yelp sounds and then silence falls again around the house. Darragh appears a moment later. The dog isn't in his hands. I'm shaking my head at him, and he shrugs. Stroking his bat has me moving up the stairs. Half of the time, I wonder how stable Darragh really is.

Upstairs has only three bedrooms. I check the front one, which holds a single bed and two lockers. The bed isn't made up. The back bedroom is used as a gym. When Darragh pokes his head around the room, he points at the weights. I don't understand what he's asking. He picks one up, and I shake my head.

"We're only scaring him," I say as quietly as I dare. He rolls his eyes and lowers the weight to the floor. The master bedroom isn't exactly master size, but compared to the rest of the house, the room is large. He's lying on his back, alone. That makes this so much easier. I move around his bed, and a snore rips from his throat. Darragh stands on the other side of him, bat resting on his shoulder.

"David, it's time to wake up." I nudge him with my bat, and he sits up, moving back into the headboard. His head snaps from me to Darragh. Raising both hands, he starts to plea.

"I don't have any money. You guys are hitting the wrong house."

Darragh moves, and David follows his movements as he makes his way to the curtains. I have no idea what Darragh is doing, but I stay focused on the message I need to deliver.

"I don't want money," I inform him and let it sink in. His eyes shoot back to me.

"What do you want?" His breathing is growing heavy now.

"You hurt a friend of mine. Neill."

He's shaking his head. "Nah, man. I swear to God, I don't even know a Neill."

I nod. Denial is always the first step.

The crack of a bat on David's leg has me grabbing for Darrah's arms.

"What are you doing?" I ask Darragh as he tries to take another swing.

David's cries are too loud. I force his head into the pillow.

"I thought we were here to beat the shit out of him." Darragh sounds confused, but I can't deal with him right now.

"David, shut the fuck up," I shout. His cries grow muffled, and I let him up slowly. He whines, drool dripping from the corner of his mouth.

"This will go a lot easier if you admit what you did."

"I swear to God. I don't know a Neill."

I push his face into the pillow before looking back at Darragh, who has Rochelle slung up on his shoulder again.

"Now you can hit him," I tell Darragh. He swings wide, and his bat connects with David's hip. I'm not sure if the crack comes from the bat or the bone, but I'm going with the bone, as he screams into the pillow.

We let him up for air once his cries settle down. I'm surprised with how long he holds out. Five hits later, and he finally admits to knowing Neill.

"Tell all your friends we're coming for them," I tell David as I land the final blow to his face. I use my fist. His eyes close, and I push him over so he's sprawled out on his back.

We leave the room, and I'm taking the stairs two at a time. "Fuck sake, Darragh," I snarl as I pass the small body of the dog.

"The fucker would have barked."

As we make it outside, the fresh air feels nice. I itch to rip off the balaclava, but I wait until I'm in the darkness of my car.

"What did you do to it?" I ask, and he pulls off his own balaclava.

"You really want to know?" He's smirking at me, and I start the car up in answer. "So when's the next job?" His excitement has him sitting forward as he sparks up a fag.

"Let's give it a few nights," I tell him, not sure if I'll bring him the next time.

"Don't you fucking bail on me," he says, and I can't stop the grin.

"Wouldn't dream of it," I tell him as we leave the estate in the rearview mirror.

"Cross my heart, I'll be better behaved the next time."

I take a quick look at him and know he's lying. When I snigger, he just shrugs.

CHAPTER TEN

CONNOR

"**W**HAT TIME IS IT?" Darragh asks.

I check my phone. "Six." He's not looking like someone who wants to go to bed. His grin has me asking, "What do you have in mind?"

He punches my shoulder as we head for the bar.

"Una, you looking for me?" Darragh teases. Una is staring into an empty fireplace. Her smile is tight. We've intruded on something.

"A drink?" He fires at her.

"Why not?"

I sit down beside her on the couch while Darragh gets the drinks.

"Are you guys just coming home?" She pulls her bare feet under her as she tucks a stray curl behind her ear.

"Yeah. Why are you up?" I ask, shrugging out of my coat.

"Couldn't sleep." She dips her head as she speaks.

"Trouble in paradise?" Darragh teases while handing me a Bud and one for Una, who snaps it from him.

"No, everything is perfect." The bite in her words tells me that it isn't perfect.

Darragh jumps across the arm of the chair, sloshing drink down his ugly brown cords.

He wipes it off with his hand and sucks the excess drink from his fingers. When he looks up to find us watching, he winks at Una.

"I thought you moved out?" he says to her.

"I thought you were in rehab?" she fires back, and that wipes the smirk clean off his face.

"I finished it," Darragh says in his defense, and Una snorts, making me grin.

"You mean you paid them off, because you're not clean."

I don't remember Una being this fiery. The idea that she knows that Darragh takes drugs makes me wonder what else she knows. She doesn't look like the carefree sister I'm used to.

"Don't take your mood out on me just because Shane is being a dick."

She stands, and so do I.

"He's playing with you," I tell Una, and she huffs before sitting back down. Any more than two members of our family in one room always turns into a referee match.

"What's this about you moving out?" I ask Una to divert the conversation to hopefully more mutual ground.

"Shane bought Deerpark Stud." My eyebrows rise, and Una smiles. "Yeah, I know," she says while taking a sip of her drink. Darragh rolls his head back and closes his eyes. He lifts his drink, nearly missing his mouth.

"Congratulations," I tell Una, tipping my bottle against hers. She gives me a shy thank you. I had no idea they even liked each other. To be moving in together is a big step. I hope it works out.

"I missed you," she admits, and a slow smile stretches across my face. "I missed you too," I tell her honestly.

"I thought you would be here sooner." Her declaration confuses me.

"How so?" I take a deep drink. Darragh's foot bounces back and forth, but he still has his eyes closed.

"I told Shane weeks ago about where you were."

The alcohol feels heavy in my stomach. "Maybe he had other stuff on," I offer, but she looks as troubled as I feel.

"Nah, he was pretty worried about you. But you're here now," she says with a chirp in her tone.

"I'm happy you're home too," Darragh says. His voice is drowsy. Una shakes her head, but she can't hide the smile.

"You love him," I tell her, getting up, and she snorts. "Right, kiddos. I'm going to hit the sack."

Darragh mumbles something. The chair will be his bed for the next few hours.

"Night, Connor," Una says sweetly, and I hope Shane treats her right. She's good blood.

***

The idea that Shane knew where I was for weeks isn't sitting right with me. It means he was either watching my movements or he was too busy to care. I'm going with the first scenario. I shower and change into fresh jeans and a shirt before carrying my socks and boots into the kitchen.

The smell of scones wafts into the hall. Mary moves quickly around the kitchen. I bend and kiss her on the cheek. She swings around, her bemused look turning into a smile.

"Connor." I haven't seen her since arriving, and her hug is nice.

"Mary, you're getting younger," I tell her, and she swipes at me playfully. Her round face and black curly hair always makes her look youthful compared to her actual fifty-plus years.

I'm sitting when she swoops in with a cup of tea.

"One sugar and some milk." She tells me with a little pat to my head. I smile up at her.

"You're the best, Mary." I take a sip, and the tea is perfect. Her robust figure moves around the kitchen, and she fills it with warmth. Her stature changes as Shane arrives. Both eyebrows rise as he nods at me. After getting his own coffee, he sits down across from me.

"You still living here?" I ask him innocently.

"This is my home."

"Oh. Just was with Una last night, and she said you bought Deerpark Stud."

He places his coffee carefully on the table. "It's being renovated at present, but we will be moving in soon."

Mary arrives with toast and places it in front of me. It's been buttered for me. "Mary, you're marriage material," I tell her, and she giggles.

Shane's face is stone. He doesn't get toast, and I eat mine slowly.

"Tell me about this guy Brian," I say.

Shane glances over his shoulder.

"She's gone," I tell him.

"No breakfast for me?"

"She doesn't seem to like you," I say back, and he shrugs.

"What about Brian?" he questions, and I'm not sure how much I should say.

"He hits that girl Ava," I admit, the toast feeling heavy in my stomach now.

Shane shrugs again. "And what about it?" He takes a sip of his coffee, and I drop my toast.

"You okay with hitting a woman?" I question, and he sits a bit straighter.

"That's not what I said. She's not our problem." He leans in now. "Look, Connor, you have one fucking job to do. So do it." He rises like it's the end of the conversation.

He pours his coffee down the sink before turning to me. "Don't even think about touching Brian either."

"Why, because of that cop?" I ask, taking a bite of my toast. It doesn't taste nice anymore, and I put the rest of the slice down.

"What cop?" The way Shane asks tells me he really doesn't know.

"The cop who's looking for the missing person. His name's Harry."

Shane's back at the table. "Lying little fucker," he tells the table.

"I take it he kept that one quiet," I say, and Shane's eyes snap up to mine.

"Why hasn't he warned the cop away from the case with the boy ?" Shane stares at me like the answer is within his reach, but then he glances away while twisting the ring on his finger—the ring that our mother bought him.

"I don't know, but I'll find out. Right now, just keep away from Brian." He gets up again, and this time, he leaves the kitchen.

Taking out my phone, I text Ava. **Want to meet up tonight?** I hit send before sliding the phone back into my pocket. After putting on my boots and socks, I grab my keys before heading outside. The fresh morning air doesn't help to clear my head. Shane not knowing about Harry being bought by Brian is bothering me.

I take a walk across the fields. I shouldn't have bothered with clean clothes. My jeans are splashed now with cow dung. I keep walking until I come to the tree line of the forest before I start to relax. I walk deep into the forest, then stop and take out my phone. I have a message from Ava.

Great. Looking forward to it.

I smile at her response before I ring the number I was given to reach my dad.

He picks up on the first ring. His Northern Irish accent makes me stiffen and relax at the same time.

"Son. I'm glad you rang."

"Everything okay ?" I ask. The fact he's glad I rang doesn't make me happy. His gladness is never good.

"We need to meet."

I nod while glancing around the forest. "Where?"

"Monaghan. Today. I'll send you the address. Then delete this number."

"Okay."

He hangs up, and my phone bleeps. Westenra Arms Hotel. 2 pm.

I arrive back at the house and change my jeans and shoes.

CHAPTER ELEVEN

AVA

WORK IS SLOW, AND I honestly don't mind. I'm keeping my hair down, and it's blocking half my face. I woke up looking worse than when I went to bed. My face has started to bruise. The makeup I applied toned it down but didn't cover it up. Thankfully, my only customers are Paul and his friends, who were playing pool when I arrived.

The glass in my hand gleams. I've been drying the same one for the last few moments. My mind keeps going to the kiss with Connor. I start on another glass as the pub doors open. I turn my back on Harry as he takes a seat at the bar. He isn't in uniform today. I don't know what he wants if he's off duty.

"Anyone serving?" he asks, and I turn with a smile on my face. The sting from my cut has my smile slipping. Harry narrows his eyes on my face, and I push my hair back behind my ear to let him see. His eyes flicker to the bar.

"A Guinness."

I don't speak as I go and get him his Guinness. Once I place it on the mat in front of him, he finally glances up at me.

"I can help you." He sounds so sincere, and I lean in. "If you help me."

His smile is soft and slimy, and I move away from him, letting my hair fall back like a curtain. People always want something in return. Domestic violence isn't enough of a reason to help someone.

I take the twenty off the bar and ring up his drink. Making myself busy down in the lounge area keeps me away from Harry. He doesn't call for me again, and when I return, he's gone, his pint left half-full.

My shift drags by; the pub only starts to pick up when I'm getting ready to leave. My shift is nearly over, and Patrick steps onto the floor at five to six and lets me go.

My bag and jacket are stashed in the lounge. Once I get them, I'm out the door. It's starting to get dark already. I don't have to hide from my landlord anymore, so I use the front door, which is next door to the pub. I still need to find a place. It's something I will have to focus on tomorrow. But right now, I need a shower and get ready for my date with Connor.

I shower and dress, and as I'm finishing up, my phone lights up on the bed.

I'm outside when you're ready. No rush.

I take one final look in the mirror. I've left all my hair down and brushed the left side behind my shoulder and down my back. The right is covering my cheek, and it tumbles down to my waist.

After smearing a bit of Vaseline on my lips, I'm good to go. My denim jacket holds my card, phone, and now keys. I don't need a bag. Locking the door behind me, I question my black trousers that look similar to my work ones, but I'm going for comfort. The flat black boots are my favorite, the sides coated in studs.

Traffic moves fast past me as I search up and down the street for Connor. I didn't ask him what he was driving. He steps out of an Audi, and that surprises me. He gives me a wave, and his lips tug up into a smile. Ducking my head, I run across the road and don't glance up until I'm at the car. Connor still watches me, and I smile while tucking my hair behind my ear. His face hardens immediately, and I let my hair fall back as I climb into the car.

"You look lovely," he says the moment he closes the door. His cologne tantalizes my senses, and I want to lean in and sniff him.

"You too." I'm grinning now as he puts on his seat belt. He does look good, in jeans that hug him and a cream top that molds itself to his wide chest.

"So where are you taking me?" I ask as he pulls out. My excitement drips into my words.

"We're nearly there," he tells me with a quick glance.

"Is our date in the car?" I really don't mind. There's something about Connor that eases me. Just being in his presence is enough.

"No." I sit back as we leave Kells and make our way off of Drumbaragh Road. Connor takes a right up into a local park. I take a peek at him under my lashes, and when he glances at me, he laughs, and it's rough and sexy as hell. Butterflies erupt in my stomach at the sound.

"I think I know what you're thinking, and that's not why we're here." He pulls up to the children's playground, and his words make me relax.

"Come on." He's getting out of the car, and I follow him. The place is deserted, but it's known as a hook-up area. That's what I thought when he pulled up, that he expected me to get dirty in the car. It's well-known for late-night antics.

We walk up the large hill toward the Spire of Llyod. I can't hide the surprise when Connor extracts a key from his pocket and uses it to open the door.

"Are you serious?" The tower is rarely ever open, and I've always wanted to stand at the top.

"A friend of a friend," he says with a smirk, and I smile.

"A friend of a friend. You have friends in high places," I tell him as he holds the door open for me. I start climbing immediately. The stone steps are steep. Lights flicker to life on the wall as Connor closes the door.

The circular stairs are making me dizzy. Rough stone bites into my palm as I run my hand along the wall.

"So do you know why someone built a lighthouse inland?" It always puzzled me.

"Some earl built it in memory of his father. It was used to watch horse racing and the hunt." I want to look at Connor. His tone is serious, and I want to see the lines on his forehead that normally accompany that serious tone. But I also don't want to fall down the stairs, so I focus on each concrete step as we continue to climb.

When we reach the top, my legs burn, and I take a moment.

"You just climbed one hundred sixty-four steps," Connor says.

I glance at him, but my surroundings capture me. I'm standing at the top of world. The only thing separating me and the outside is a pane of glass that runs in a full circle around the top of the tower.

"Wow." It's breathtaking, and I move closer to the glass. Looking at the ground makes me want to take a step back.

"Yeah, I like coming here to think."

"I would too," I answer, not looking away from the scene before us. Green fields stretch out, cut up by trees and small stripes of gray concrete. Car lights flash in the distance. Closing one eye, I cover a moving car with my finger.

"I'm sorry for leaving you last night." Connor's words are close. He's right behind me, and I shiver. My eyes clash with his in the glass.

"Don't be. I was fine," I tell his reflection.

"I hate that he hurt you." When he speaks, the lines appear on his forehead. He looks conflicted now, and I turn around so I can see him properly. His brown eyes flicker to my lips, and I wet them.

His fingers reach out and brush my damaged cheek. Closing my eyes, my skin warms, and I can almost feel it heal with his touch.

"My mother was a strong woman. I could never understand her staying." My eyes snap open at Connor's words. I hate that I'm a reminder of what his mother suffered. I'm not like her. I'm not a victim of domestic abuse. This is different. I'm not staying. I'm not allowing myself to be someone's punch bag. I went to the guards. He just bought them off.

"As I got older, I learned that she stayed for her children. She hid it so well." His smile carries no happiness. There's a weight on his shoulders that I want to lift off.

"She was a good mother," I tell him, and his eyes rest on me.

"She was stupid." His brows furrow as he speaks harshly, and there it is. He thinks I'm stupid too.

"I'm sorry about your mom, Connor, but I'm not her." I don't want to be a ghost of something so painful for him. My words cause him to take a step back while widening his eyes.

"I know you're not. I just... I want to beat the shit out of Brian."

I want him to beat the shit out of Brian too. I allow myself to picture that, and a smile tugs at my lips before reality comes crashing back in.

"I know, but you'd end up hurt worse than him, and I don't want that." My confession surprises me. I don't know Connor, but I don't want to see him hurt.

He takes a step toward me as his lips pull into a smile.

This time, he takes my face with both hands, his eyes searching mine. I don't hesitate to rise on tippy-toes and kiss him. His lips are warm and moist, and I moan into his mouth as he pulls me closer to him. His body is flush against mine. We're moving, and my back touches a cold surface. My tongue slips easily into his mouth and his moves into mine. His moan has me pushing myself harder against him.

His large palm brushes my left breast. Hard nipples push against my black top, and I shift my body so his fingers brush my nipples. Wetness pools between my legs, and I want him so bad. My fingers are digging into his shoulders as I try to move him closer. His bulge brushes my sensitive area, and I'm pushing off his jacket, unbuttoning his shirt, and he isn't stopping me. Opening my eyes, I take in his tanned skin, smooth and muscular. Our kiss is broken, and his deep brown eyes have me holding my breath. The intensity in his eyes nearly undoes me.

I'm shrugging out of my jacket, and when I pull my top over my head, it lands in the pile of growing clothes on the floor. His large hand sinks into my hair as his lips touch mine again. My fingers are greedy and move to the band of his trousers. I want them off. I'm fumbling with his jeans when he pauses, his forehead leaning against mine.

"I don't want to stop, but I'm giving you a fair warning. We're surrounded by glass, and the lights are on so…"

I wish he hadn't reminded me. I'm nodding, trying to gather myself, but I keep my eyes closed as I lick my lips.

He hasn't moved as he waits for me to give the green light. But as much as I want this, I don't want an audience.

"Can you pass me my top?" I ask as my way of saying we're stopping this. Connor lets out a breath that brushes my face, and when he opens his eyes, my stomach jumps. Biting my lip, I force myself to stay still and not close the distance between us. The coldness is instant when Connor steps away and hands me my top. I pull it on quickly and take my jacket. Connor pulls on his shirt, and I watch him button it up. He glances up at me from under thick black lashes. The tug of his lips has me smiling too.

My body is still singing. My blood burns hot, so I go back to staring at the view. I need to bring my temperature and hormone levels down before I change my mind. The room allows you to walk a full circle, and it's just beautiful. Cars have started to arrive at the park, and it's no secret what everyone is doing. Now I envy them. They don't have to stop.

I end up sitting down, my knees brushing the glass. I know this opportunity won't come around again, so I try to take it all in. A new memory. Connor joins me, his leg brushing mine, and I wonder if he sat so close on purpose.

"Someone, somewhere, at this exact moment, is looking at the same sky," I tell Connor's reflection.

"Right now, I'm the only person in the world that's looking at you."

My eyes snap to him. His words burn my throat. It's the way he says it that has my stomach flipping. Like looking at me matters. Like I matter.

His kiss is featherlight. He brushes it gently across my lips before leaning back out and focusing on the view in front of us, like he didn't just say the most amazing thing.

CHAPTER TWELVE

CONNOR

"Wake up." I open one eye and stare up at Darragh. "This better be important," I tell him. My mind is still stuck on Ava. With Darragh sitting on my bed and my mind going to Ava, I sit up and rub my face.

"It's Finn's birthday today."

Rubbing my eyes, I reach for my phone. It's ten in the morning. It feels like the middle of the night with how tired I am.

"I think we should all go to the lake together. Like the old days." There's a pleading in Darragh's voice that's not just for Finn. I'm awake now, the longing on his face obvious.

"Okay, but it's your birthday too," I say and get a punch to the arm for agreeing and mentioning his birthday. Darragh isn't one for celebrating his own birthday. He jumps off the bed before I can say any more.

"Going to wake the dragon," he tells me with a grin.

"Who, Shane or Liam?" I ask, and his laughter lingers in my room after he leaves.

My head dips to my shoulder. I can smell Ava's perfume on me. Last night, we spent time talking in the tower before getting food. She offered for me to come upstairs, but I knew if I did, I wouldn't leave. I wasn't sure if I was stupid or what, but with the cut on her face, I wanted it to heal first, or else I felt I was taking advantage.

I'm dressed when Darragh sticks his head in my room door.

"I got a yes out of Shane," he says, and that clarifies who the dragon is.

"Off to wake sleeping beauty," he updates me before leaving again.

Finn is in the kitchen when I arrive. "Happy Birthday," I wish him while getting a cup of tea. "I hear we're all going to the lake."

"Yeah, can't wait." Finn sounds anything but excited, but his eyes don't lie.

"Everyone is coming," Darragh announces as I sit down. He opts for sitting on the table.

"You're telling me you convinced Liam?" Finn sounds as skeptical as I feel.

"I have a way of convincing people."

"Yeah, hammering on and on until we agree." Shane arrives in the kitchen, and Darragh jumps off the table.

"You out last night?" Finn asks me.

I stare at him through bleary eyes. I feel like I was drinking, but I wasn't. "Work, not pleasure," I tell him. My stomach tightens with guilt at my words.

Darragh arrives back to the table with a bowl of cornflakes. He talks while eating, and it's hard to focus.

"So there are rules about today."

Shane sits across from Darragh with toast and a coffee. "Swallow your food first. I don't need to see what's in your mouth."

"Brothers," Liam greets us, and I flicker him a glance over my shoulder.

"Yep, he's in a suit," I say, and Finn snorts a laugh.

"Are you going to the lake in that?" I ask before taking a sip of my tea.

Liam joins us, and I realize this is the first time in years that we've all sat at a table together.

"Does it bother you?" The question is said as he sits down.

"No," I answer with a shrug.

"It bothers me. I think we should all wear T-shirts and shorts," Darragh shoots out.

"It's freezing outside." Shane's tone is low.

"And I like my suit," Liam finishes off.

I grin at Finn, and he smirks back.

"So we are doing this?" Darragh sits back up on the table. Liam pauses eating his toast to stare at Darragh, but he doesn't notice.

Darragh bobbles his head to music we can't hear, and I wonder for the hundredth time if he's high. I can't blame him if he is.

"I'll ride with Connor," Finn says. I'm fine with Finn riding with me.

"We're going on foot," Darragh says.

Shane's head snaps up from his phone. "I just bought these shoes."

"Change them," I tell him, and he glares at me.

"It's Finn's decision," Liam speaks up, but he's also now focused on his phone.

I shake my head at Finn. Walking to the lake sounds painful.

"Come on, Finn. It will be like old times." Darragh's like a dog with a bone, and I can see when Finn gives in before he even says yes.

"I'm just making a call before we leave." I take my mug of tea with me outside. I glance back into the kitchen as my phone rings; it's odd to see them all still sitting at the table.

When he answers, I say, "Russell, how did you get on with Neill's house?"

"Got it sealed. But they did a number on his house. Haven't seen Neill around. Is he okay?"

"Yeah, they broke his fingers and nose."

"Fuckers. Does he know who did it?"

"He couldn't get a clear look at them."

"Pity," Russell responds. I check over my shoulder to make sure no one is listening.

"You still got that place in Headfort Demesne?" I ask.

"Yeah, you looking to rent?"

"No. It's for a friend." I'm not sure what Ava is, but she's more than a friend.

"Look, Connor, it's a private establishment. I can't have any guys in that party and stuff."

"It's a girl. She's a hard worker and will keep the place clean. No partying." There's a brief pause.

"Okay, it's fifteen hundred a month, and a month's deposit."

I glance in the window to see everyone still sitting around the table. "No deposit and tell her it's four hundred a month. I'll cover the rest."

"She more than a friend?"

"Have we got a deal?" I ask.

"Yeah, we've got a deal."

"Thanks, Russell. I'll be in touch."

I arrive back into a fight between Darragh and Finn. I'm not sure what it's about, but Liam barks a warning and silence falls. Shane glances up at me as I place my cup in the sink.

"What's going on?" I ask, and Darragh jumps off the table.

"I'm always wrong."

"You're always high," Finn fires back.

Shane rises, slipping his phone into his back pocket. "Ladies, really? Is this necessary?"

"Can we go and get this done and over with?" Finn's dry tone is how I feel about this, but for him, I'll go.

"Give me a second." Darragh is out the door, a grin back on his face. His recent anger is gone.

We don't have long to wait before Darragh arrives with a backpack that he slings over his back. No one asks what's in it. I think we all have a fair idea.

Darragh takes the lead, and we follow him. I grin when he steps into the field. We aren't taking the main road. He's taking the shortcut that we all took as kids. We're no longer the young brothers with scrapped knees and ideas about wanting to be gangsters. Now we're all grown, scared, and I'm not sure if we know how to be anything else but gangsters.

Liam looks the most ridiculous out of us all, trekking across a field in a suit.

"Remember that time Liam wore the red T-shirt," Darragh starts.

"Yeah and the bull chased him," Finn finished, laughter in his voice. Shane snorts in front of me, and I can't stop the grin that spreads across my face.

"He was like Forest Gump," I say, and Shane smirks across at me.

"He was slipping and sliding." Darragh's laughing now, and Liam looks across at him.

"Thank you for that, Darragh," Liam says with a smile.

"You are very welcome." Darragh walks backward so he can look at us all. The smile seems permanently on his face. Maybe he's right being so carefree. Maybe the rest of us are way too uptight.

"Oh, I have a good one. Remember when Connor tried to ride the sheep?" I nearly trip at Darragh's words, and he roars with laughter.

"Don't say it like that. I tried to get up on its back," I defend. Finn joins in with Darragh's laughter. Yeah, that didn't sound any better.

Now Shane snorts. "I was small enough to ride it."

"Fuck's sake, you know what I mean. I was young enough, and it was like a little horse." My defenses starts to dwindle, and I join their laughter. It doesn't matter what I say; it's all coming out wrong.

Darragh reminisces about our childhood, and before we know it, we're at the lake. The walk seemed so much quicker than it did when we were kids.

The lake doesn't look as large and overbearing as it once was. As a kid, it was an ocean.

Darragh unzips his bag and takes out two bottles of JD. I take one from him and unscrew the cap. It burns as it makes a path down my throat. I pass it to Liamm who takes a deep swallow.

"I've missed this place," I tell the lake. It reminds me of Mom. She would bring us here and let us swim when we were too young to venture off by ourselves.

Liam moves closer to the lake, hands in his pockets as he peers in.

"Me too," Finn says, and I watch Darragh drop the bag, and he's running toward Liam, each step filled with the excitement of a child. He doesn't just knock Liam into the lake; he goes over the edge with him. Finn, Shane, and myself are peering in, warily looking at each other. I have no intentions of shoving anyone in.

"I just got a new phone," Shane says.

"Me too," I counter.

"I hate water." Finn takes a step back.

Liam surfaces, along with Darragh. Liam doesn't make a sound when he breaks through the water. He swims back toward us, his strokes precise. He looks like a professional swimmer, not someone who was just pegged into a lake while wearing a suit.

Darragh releases a yelp of excitement. "Come in. It's warm," he tells the rest of us as Liam reaches the side and drags himself out of the lake. Darragh's lips rattle together.

"I'll pass," I tell him. I go back to the backpack and retrieve the bottle of JD. Sitting on the ground, I take a deep swallow. Liam's stripping off, placing his suit jacket neatly on a bush.

"You're a moron," Shane barks at Darragh, but his words hold amusement. Shane's phone starts to ring. He takes it out and flickers a glance at Liam.

"It's Dad," he says before answering.

"Don't answer that." Darragh's panicked words have the other shoe falling.

"Why would I not answer it?" Shane surprisingly doesn't answer it straight away, and Darragh pulls himself over the side of the lake.

"Just let me explain first."

"What have you done?" Liam asks, and the way the three boys approach him with such exasperation says that Darragh gets into more trouble than he used to. Shane's phone stops ringing, but Finn's starts right away.

"You've got ten seconds before I answer this." Finn holds up his phone to Darragh. I take another drink and stay where I am. My phone doesn't ring. I've recently changed my number. Liam's phone won't be ringing after going for a swim in the lake, and neither will Darragh's. I wonder now if that's why he threw himself and Liam into the lake.

"I got a tip-off that the guards were going to arrest me today." Darragh drips water around his feet as he glares at his brothers like somehow this is their fault.

"What did you do?" Liam asks again.

"Siobhan's aunt—they found my DNA on a cigarette." Shane shakes his head and steps away from Darragh.

"Did I not tell you to pick them up?" Shane's barking at Finn, who's turned pale.

"Don't start pointing the finger at me," he shouts back. Darragh takes a box of fags out of his shirt pocket. Water pours from the box before he throws them on the ground.

"Who tipped you off?" I ask, and all eyes fall on me.

His eyes shift to Shane before returning to me. "Brian. He has a guard paid off. Heard they were coming for me."

"They can't do anything with just a cigarette butt. Someone could have carried it into her house on their shoe." Shane tells this to Liam like if he can explain it away, it will make all this stop.

"This wasn't even about my birthday," Finn says to Darragh, who rest on his hunkers.

"It was a bit of both." Darragh's voice is low, but I catch his words.

"Oh, so my birthday and the fact you're being arrested for murder. Two birds with one stone. Is that it, Darragh?" Darragh's up, fists clenched, and I'm rising. Darragh sees my movements and takes a step away from Finn.

I'm standing now as Shane's phone rings again. He answers, and the one-sided conversation is hard to follow. His final question has me watching Shane. "What should we do?" he asks Michael. Shane nods into the phone.

"Okay. Yeah." Darragh is holding his breath as Shane turns to him.

"I know he wants you to hand me over to them."

"It wasn't just a fag butt. Your fingerprints were found in her bedroom. What were you doing in her room?"

Finn runs his hands through his hair and turns away from Darragh and Shane. "Oh my fucking God."

"Siobhan's going to know."

"Calm down," Liam tells Finn in a very calming voice, and I find myself taking a step closer to Finn.

"She was asleep, so I woke her up." Darragh shrugs, but the way he won't hold anyone's eyes tells me he's hiding something.

"You didn't rape her?" I ask the question that everyone is thinking.

"Fuck off." The disgust in Darragh's voice gives me the answer. Still, his actions are creepy as fuck.

"What do I do?" he asks Liam.

"You stay calm. You don't say a word. Don't speak. My lawyer will deal with it." Finn glances up at me, the weight of the world on his shoulders. He walks to me and picks up the bottle of JD. He drinks it until he needs air.

"I'm sorry, lad," I tell the side of his face. This is some fucking mess. But I have all the faith in Liam that he will get Darragh out of this.

Shane gives Liam his phone so he can make his call. Sirens blare in the distance, and Darragh pales, moving toward Liam, like he offers some sort of protection.

"I told Dad to tell them where we are. Better here than at the house."

"You're going to let them arrest me?"

"You killed someone, you little fucker, so be a man," I tell him. I shouldn't have said it out loud. But he's pissing me off, running from one brother to another.

"Fuck you. You're not even part of this family."

I laugh at his words, even though they sting. "Get used to the smell of metal bars." My words have him charging me. Two Gardaí cars appear as I take Darragh to the ground.

I'm holding him down when they jump from the cars. I recognize Harry but don't want him to recognize me, so I let Darragh go and try to keep my face hidden.

"Darragh O'Reagan, you're under arrest for the murder of Ruth Walsh. You have the right to remain silent. If you do say anything, what you say can be used against you in a court of law." Harry is the arresting officer and pulls Darragh off the ground while placing cuffs on him. "You have the right to consult with a lawyer and have that lawyer present during any questioning. If you cannot afford a lawyer, one will be appointed to you."

No one speaks as Darragh is placed in the back of the Gardaí car. We watch as the two cars pull out onto the road, and once they leave, I turn to Finn.

"Happy Birthday."

CHAPTER THIRTEEN

AVA

How the hell did I gather so much crap? I'm packing a bookshelf. It's small and filled with books and some figurines and picture frames. I feel like I'm packing forever. When I finally wrap the last item, which happens to be a small statue of the Virgin Mary, my bell rings. The statue was previously stashed behind a picture. My nan had given it to me for protection, but I wasn't overly fond of displaying it.

"Hello." I take the receiver away from my face; something sticky is on the side and is now on my cheek.

"Ava, it's Harry."

I want to hang up the phone. "What do you want?" I ask.

"Just a minute." I glance around my apartment. I don't want him here in my personal space, but it won't be mine for much longer. I buzz him in and unlock the front door. My heart hammers as his footsteps echo in the hallway. He appears and gives me a nod as he climbs the last few steps.

I fold my arms across my chest and stay standing in the doorway. "What?" I snap.

Harry glances behind him and even moves a few feet back so he can look up at the stairs to the next floor.

"Just a minute, please."

Against my better judgment, I let him in. I don't like that he's in uniform. He closes the door as we enter the sitting room. He doesn't sit but removes his hat, and now I'm sitting because my mind is going to Nan. Something is wrong. When they remove their hats, it's delivering bad news. I've seen it in every movie. My hand flutters to my throat.

"I just want to talk," Harry says, and my heart flutters before it starts to settle.

Nan is fine, I tell myself.

"I can't help you," he says, "because Brian would target my family."

"Then what are you doing here?"

"I want to help, Ava." Harry's cheeks are tinted with a bright pink.

"Then let me file the complaint against him. He hasn't just hit me once." I'm shouting and remind myself that I have neighbors. Taking a deep, calming breath, I run my hands down the leg of my tracksuit bottoms.

"I can't. But you could do something else." He pauses, his eyes now taking in my living space, and it feels so invasive.

"Which is?" I bark, pulling him back to me.

"You could help us. Brian deals drugs, but we can't pin him down. If you could find something on him, he would be locked up for a long time."

I laugh humorlessly. "You want me to wear a wire?" I ask.

Harry grins, and I want to ask him what's so fucking amusing. "No, just get close to him and maybe let us know if anything arises."

"You want me to get close to someone who's hit me." I stand. I want him out of my apartment.

"Ava, I know he hurt you, but Brian hurts a lot of people who can't do anything about it. He likes you. You can do something."

I can't hold Harry's eye. He's right. Maybe I could get close to Brian, but it feels like a really stupid thing to do. "I'll think about it," I tell Harry and am surprised when he nods.

"Thank you." He places his hat back on his head and leaves.

After Harry leaves, I continue packing, but my mind is a jumbled mess. The missing man niggles at me now. What if something bad happened to him? What if telling the guards that I saw Brian with him could be enough to put him behind bars? I didn't get a good look at the other guy.

Small pieces of glass spray across the floor as the bite to my finger has me putting my finger in my mouth. Crap. A small Galway Crystal holder that my nan got me is in a million pieces on the floor. The tang of metal in my mouth has me removing my finger and assessing it. It's not deep, but it's like a paper cut. The pain is intense.

I clean up and don't return to packing. After sticking a Band-Aid on my finger and grabbing my jacket and bag, I make my way to the Gardaí station.

A *bangharda* is at the counter. They're worse than the men. The glass that divides stays sealed as she glances up but returns to whatever she's doing under the desk. So I take a seat. My stomach won't settle. I withheld information, and now saying that I did so because Harry wouldn't allow me to press charges against Brian just doesn't seem like an option. My phone vibrates in my pocket, and I take it out as the bangharda pulls open the window.

"Next," she barks, but I'm the only one here. She gives me a lazy look, and I answer the phone. She can wait.

"Hi," he says.

"Hi to you too." I smile at his voice. The Bangharda is watching me, so I take my call outside, telling Connor to give me a second. He holds until the fresh air flitters across my face. "Sorry. I'm up here at the guards."

"Is everything okay?" His words are rushed, and I want to ease him immediately.

"Yeah, nothing has happened," I tell him.

"Good. Are you there to press charges against Brian?" he asks.

I want to say yes, but pressing charges against Brian just doesn't seem like an option.

"No. It's about something else. Something I saw." The line is silent. "Connor?" I question, thinking he must have gone.

"Yeah, sorry. I'm here. What do you mean something you saw?"

I chew my lip now. "There's a missing person, and he was in Smyth's with Brian and another man. I think I should tell them what I saw."

"Is this the picture that Harry was showing you?" Connor sounds odd.

"Yeah."

"Ava, I know you think you are doing good, but why didn't you tell the guards before? You'll get into trouble."

I stop chewing my lip when I taste blood. "I thought of that, but I could say that I just remembered." Okay, that sounded lame. I glance back at the door. The Bangharda is out fixing the leaflets.

"I just want it off my conscious," I admit to Connor.

"I know, but they won't care. You withheld information. You will be in trouble for obstructing their investigation. Maybe what you saw was nothing. That guy is probably at some wild party." Connor did have a point, but yet, someone was looking for him, his family. Maybe my information that he was drunk and left with two guys wouldn't do any good.

"Yeah, you're right," I tell Connor, stepping away from the Gardaí station and making my way back down the road.

"I just worry about you," he says, and I pause as the traffic moves past me. Why do his words hold guilt?

"Seriously, don't worry about me. I can take care of myself."

A short relieved laugh from Connor has me smiling.

"Will I be seeing you later?" I ask, and he pauses.

"I'm not sure. We have a bit of a family situation at the moment, but I'll try my best."

I'm slightly disappointed, but I don't say that. "Okay."

"I'll contact you later."

I nod into the phone. "Yeah, that's cool."

"Where are you now?" he asks, and I glance around me.

"I'm at my door. Why?" I ask, expecting him to suddenly appear.

"Just wanted to make sure you got home safe."

He's so sweet. I turn the key in the door. "I'm inside now," I tell him, and he seems content when he says goodbye.

I've got no one waiting for me when I get upstairs. Ringing Nan for the third time has alarm bells going off in my head. Even when Harry was here, she was all I could think about. Her not answering isn't normal, but I have work in ten minutes. Going to the Gardaí station and having Harry here burned through my packing time. I still have so much to do.

***

I'm on the early shift again, so it's quiet.

Patrick appears out of the back. "Just going to do the lodgments."

"No problem," I tell him, and he leaves. The bank is only a few doors down, so he's never long. I take out my phone and ring my nan again. My stomach tightens when she doesn't pick up.

"A pint when you're ready," Paul says.

I stuff my phone in my pocket and give Paul a smile. "Coming right up," I tell him. Placing the pint in front of him, I can see the question in his eyes before he asks me.

"Are you alright?" His eyes linger on my face. I completely forgot about it.

"Oh, this?" I point at my face. "Hit myself with a lamp while packing," I tell him, and he grins.

"Jesus, you gave yourself some smack."

I take the twenty. "I know."

"You need to be a bit more careful," a voice says.

My hand stills over the till, but I quickly remember myself and get Paul his change. I don't look at Brian as he leans across the bar. But he's here, and I hate him for how he's making me feel.

"What the hell do you want?" I can't take much more of him. His smile falls, and my voice carries across the bar. There seems to be a stillness around us, and his blue eyes turn cold.

"How's your nan?"

The question has me locking my knees together, and I'm shaking my head. "No."

"What's wrong, Ava?" The way Brian asks has me moving toward the end of the bar. Patrick arrives in the door, and his eyes flicker from Brian to me.

"Patrick, can I leave early today?" I ask quickly, already grabbing my bag and jacket.

"Yeah, of course. Is everything okay?" His worry is genuine.

"She's fine. I've got it," Brian says, reaching his arm toward me as I come from around the bar. But I'm not pretending.

"Don't touch me. What did you do to her?" I shout, and he steps in closer.

"Shut the fuck up, Ava."

"You promised me you wouldn't touch her." My low words are accompanied by tears. Brian is toe to toe with me now, his breath on my bruised cheek.

"You promised me a second chance."

If I had the courage, I would strike him, but I don't. I move around him and out the door.

"Ava." My name bounces off the cobbled stone pavement, and I don't look back. Instead, I ring Connor, but it goes to voice mail.

"Ava." Brian's voice is more distant now when I wave down a cab and give the driver directions to my nan's house.

CHAPTER FOURTEEN

CONNOR

"WHAT'S TAKING SO LONG?" Finn asks. I can't seem to keep him still. He's pacing the library as we wait for word on Darragh.

"They can hold him for forty-eight hours," I remind Finn. "Liam has someone working on it. Trust me, when the forty-eight hours are up, he will be home."

He rubs his face. "What do I say to Siobhan when she asks?"

I have no clue. "Play dumb," I offer lamely. I wouldn't want to be in his situation.

Shane arrives in the room, his eyes narrowing on Finn, and it's pissing me off how everyone is blaming Finn for Darragh's actions.

"Any word?" I ask Shane, and his head snaps to me. He walks deeper into the room.

"He's staying quiet. The lawyer is with him now. We hope to have him out in a few hours."

"Where were you that night?" he asks Finn, who looks up at him while scratching his eyebrow.

"With you. I helped you."

"You're a moron. If the guards ask, where were you?"

"Shane, just calm down," I tell him, and Finn rises.

"It's fine, Connor. I was with Siobhan, and then I came and picked up Darragh from a party."

Shane nods. "Try to remember that."

"Try not to be such a dick," I tell him as he leaves. He glares at me quickly before turning the corner. Finn needs to start standing up to Shane and Liam. They treat him like they always have, I suppose—their baby brother who they can boss around. I need to return a call to Ava. That's another problem. Her being at the Gardaí station today was too close for comfort.

"I'll be back in a minute," I tell Finn, who is sitting back down. He just nods as I leave the room.

She answers on the first ring. "Ava, sorry I missed your call."

"I can't talk right now." She sounds upset, and all I can think of is that she changed her mind and is making a statement against Shane.

"Where are you?" I ask, boring a hole into the wall.

"At the hospital. I'm okay. It's my nan."

"What hospital?"

"Navan. She's going to be fine, but can I give you a call later?" she asks, and I hate her being alone up there, knowing that she has no family.

"Sure. Chat soon," I tell her, and the call ends. I exhale a breath.

"You okay if I tip out for a while?" I ask Finn, just sticking my head in the door. There isn't much we can do now—only wait for news.

"Yeah, I think I need to get out too."

I nod. He's right to get out. Sitting here will drive him mad.

***

Despite Ava saying not to, I go to the hospital anyway. I go to reception to ask where Ava's nan is, but I don't know her name. Ava's last name is Smith, but I'm sure if it's her nan's is the same.

I sit down on one of the plastic chairs that are designed to break your back and send her a text. **I'm in the hospital at reception.**

While waiting, I send a text to Neill. **Was the message delivered?**

"Connor." I glance up into the emerald green eyes that are filled with worry. "You didn't have to come." She looks pale.

I rise, unsure what to do. I stuff my phone into my pocket and leave my hands in them too. "I wanted to make sure you're okay."

She smiles. "Let's get a coffee."

"Coffee sounds good. That would make this our third date." Her smile grows, and I'm smiling too.

The coffee shop is tiny. Ten tables fill the space, all empty. Ava orders two coffees and tells me to grab a table. I would prefer to be the one getting the coffees, but I think she needs to do something right now.

She lets out a shaky breath, and the tremble in her hands shakes our mugs. When she sets them on the table, I cover her hand with mine, making her look at me.

"No matter what, it's going to be okay," I tell her, and her eyes shine with unshed tears as she sits down.

"It's my fault." She swallows and stares at the ceiling, as if the emotion will somehow slide back down her throat.

"It's okay, Ava." I squeeze her hand, making her look at me. Tears stream down her face.

"I told Brian I would give him a second chance, just to keep him happy. But he knew I was lying. He saw me with you." She swallows again, and I'm holding my breath. I'm going to fucking kill him.

"He hurt her. She's the sweetest woman ever, and he hurt her." Her words turn angry. Her tears continue to roll, and I move my chair so I can pull hers close to mine. She's in my arms, spilling her sorrow on my top, and with each tear that falls, I promise I will take that from Brian.

Her sobs subside, and she leans out. "Sorry, I'm a mess. You shouldn't have come."

I hand her a white napkin that sits on the table. "I want to be here," I tell her, and she takes it and wipes her face. She's beautiful. Her eyes still glisten, but the determination on her face tells me she won't cry anymore.

"Is there any chance I get to meet this famous woman?" When I ask, she barks a short laugh while wiping under her eyes.

"I've told her about you. But be warned, she's fierce."

"I'm sure I can handle her," I tell Ava as I pour milk and one sugar into both our coffees. She's pretty shaken up. Each time she drinks from her coffee, her hands rattle, and something in me keeps stirring and getting larger. I hurt people just to hurt them, but this feels different. I want to hurt Brian so he can never hurt Ava again.

"I hope I didn't pull you away from anything."

"I was just hanging out with my brother," I tell the half-truth.

"You've a brother?" She seems surprised, but I've never spoken of them. I'm not meant to get close. I'm here for a job.

"I've five half brothers and a stepsister," I tell her, and she nearly chokes on her coffee, making me smile.

"Wow, that's a huge family. Do you get on with them all?"

Now I drink my coffee before answering. "I do with three of them. Finn and Darragh are twins, but we've always been close, and my other brother Bernard I get on with," I answer. My stomach twists at the thought of Bernard. I hoped the next time I rang Dad, he would tell me that Bernard was home.

"And the rest?" This really seems to have taken her mind off her nan, but now I feel like I'm dancing around the truth, and it's getting dangerous. But their names won't do any harm.

"Shane and Liam are the older two, so I don't exactly see eye to eye with them."

"And your stepsister?"

"She's great. Maybe you'll meet her someday." The moment the words are out of my mouth, the more unlikely that actual scenario seems. Ava meeting Una would mean her meeting Shane.

"Will we go in?" I ask her. This conversation has veered onto a path I don't want to go down. She nods and leads me to her nan's room.

The little old lady in bed is exactly what I pictured. Ava did her justice. I feel scruffy now as I rub my jaw.

"Nan, this is Connor." Ava's voice shakes slightly, and I try not to lean in too close to her nan. I don't want to scare her after her being attacked. A large white bandage is wrapped around her head, which is the only visible sign that she was hurt.

"Lovely to meet you," I tell her, reaching out my hand, and she takes it. Her grip is firm and warm.

"What are your intentions with my granddaughter?" I'm nodding and trying not to grin at the ferocity in her words and the hold she has on me.

"Nan, please," Ava says while sitting down on the side of the bed.

"I like your granddaughter," I tell her honestly, and she nods.

Blue beady eyes pierce me as she continues to grip my hand. "Don't think you can hang your hat and leave it there."

"Oh my God, Nan." Ava sounds mortified, and I want to smile. I'm not sure what that statement means, but Ava's humiliation is telling me it's sexual.

"I never leave my hat behind." Both her eyebrows rise up to her hairline, and she finally releases my hand.

"So, where are you from?"

I take a moment to glance at Ava, whose face is stark red, and I smile. "Kingscourt area."

"I've relations buried down there. Do you know John Mc-Cluskey?"

"I can't say I do," I answer.

Ava's nan asks me lots of questions, much to Ava's embarrassment, but I soon see that her nan is doing it because she knows Ava's embarrassed. She's enjoying it. Ava's right. Her nan is fierce, but I love her strength. Visiting time is almost up when she asks Ava to give us a moment.

"Not a hope." Ava's answer is immediate.

"It's only a minute," I tell Ava, and her eyes widen.

"Why are you encouraging her?" she asks, but she rises.

"Fine, whatever she says is on you," she says to me. I smile as she leaves, but not before she plants a kiss on her grandmother's cheek.

Nan speaks while staring after Ava. "She's a good kid. Had a hard life." It's like the walls fall down, and the pain that I didn't notice before is evident now on her face. The paleness of her skin has me leaning in.

"Shall I get a nurse?"

"No. She can't be left alone. Brian, her previous boyfriend, hit her, and he'll do it again." Her fear for Ava is clouding her eyes.

"I won't leave her alone." I make the promise before she asks, and her body seems to sink deeper into the pillows.

"She has no one in this world. Only me." She speaks to the ceiling before fixing me with a hard gaze. "You will have to mind her until I get out."

"I will," I tell her, and she nods.

"Now, here she comes. Just laugh."

And I do. Some of my laughter is real.

"What's so funny?" Ava folds her arms gently across her chest, but her emerald eyes sparkle.

"Mind your business," Nan tells her. "Now go on. Go home and rest, child." She reaches out an arm to Ava, and Ava steps into her embrace. I put the stool back against the wall and stand, not sure if I should go.

"Don't you renege on your promise," she warns me.

"Oh my God, Nan! What did you make him promise?" Ava sounds seriously worried.

"She's joking," I tell Ava, and she relaxes. Before we leave, I lean in and place a soft kiss on Ava's nan's cheek. "I'll take care of her," I whisper before leaning out, and her eyes fog up.

"Go on," she barks while looking away, not wanting us to see her cry. Ava doesn't want to leave, but when I entwine our fingers, she leaves with me.

She doesn't speak as we make our way out in the parking lot. "I can't go home." Her voice is low, and she looks at me from under her lashes. I would have her stay with me, only the whole Shane thing would be a mess.

"Yeah, I know. I have a friend who is looking for a tenant for his apartment. You could stay there tonight, see if you like the place. If you do, it's yours." Her eyes widen.

"Seriously?" she asks, and I grin.

"Yeah. Just let me ring him."

She tugs my hand, stopping me from walking any further. When I look down at her, I don't expect her to be so close.

"Thank you." She steps into me and rises on her tippy toes. Gently, she plants a soft warm kiss on my lips. The kiss doesn't last long enough.

"You're welcome." I'm staring into emerald eyes that are becoming familiar, and that is dangerous.

***

Russell stays true to his word. A set of keys are left with the security when we check into Headfort Demesne. Ava hasn't said anything since we left her apartment. I brought her back so she could pack some clothes.

The car glides into the driveaway, and I move past the white barrier that is lowered behind us.

"Okay, straight up. I can't afford this place."

I was waiting for that. It's a gorgeous space, with courtyards and private security. You bet you paid through the nose for it.

"You don't even know how much it is yet," I tell Ava as I park, and she snorts.

"I know it's out of my budget."

I don't answer her but get out of the car and grab her two bags. She follows me to number two. The red shutters on the windows are closed. Russell did tell me that they need to be opened.

"You go on in and check the place out. I'll just get the shutters open." I place the keys in Ava's hands, and she stares at them.

"I don't want to go in." Now she has my attention.

"Why?"

"I know I'm going to fall in love with the place, and then I can't keep it." She shuffles the keys from one hand to the other. I snatch them from her open hand and enter the apartment. It's dark with the shutters closed over, but immediately, I can feel the warmth.

Ava still stands outside the door, pouting. "If you don't come in, I'll carry you in," I threaten and laugh when she doesn't move. I take a step toward her, and she holds her hands up.

"Fine, I'm coming in."

I watch her take in each room. The place is spotless. All the furniture is white, and everything looks brand new. The hardwood floors under our feet are polished.

"A four-poster bed," I say when we enter the bedroom. Ava walks to the bed and holds one of the banisters before walking around the other side.

"It's a big bed," she tells me, and I take a step into the room, hoping I'm not mistaking her invitation.

"Shall I get my tape, and we can measure it?" I ask, and she bursts out laughing.

She's so alive when she laughs. The noise that leaves her lips is musical, but it's how it makes her eyes shine and her cheeks glow. Perfection.

I take another step into the room and pretend to be really examining the bed. "I like the floral duvet cover," I tell her, and she's still smiling, still flushed.

"I bet it's comfortable," I say, and she moves closer, kneeling on the bed. She does a half jump.

"It's soft." I use my hands, pushing them deep into the mattress.

"Very soft," I say as I move around the bed toward her. She's still kneeling, but her eyes track me.

I stop when I'm directly behind her, leaning in; I place a kiss on her neck. Her head rolls back, giving me more access to her.

"You smell lovely," I tell her. Her perfume fills the air as I remove her top. The red bra she wears is full, and my jeans tighten. My lips touch her shoulder, and she shivers under me. Her tanned skin is soft and perfect. My hands trail down her front until I brush her breasts. Her moans are a drug that I can't get enough of.

Taking her ear lobe in between my teeth, I suck and bite softly. Her nipples harden in my hands. She's moving under me, growing impatient, so I let her turn and face me. Her arm wraps around my neck as she pulls me to her lips. We move onto the bed, Ava taking the lead now. When her lips brush my neck, the slight pinch of pain mixed with pleasure zooms through my body.

I'm shrugging off my jacket and break the kiss to pull my shirt off over my head. Ava's eyes roam my chest, and she flickers a hungry gaze up at me before she pulls me back down on top of her. Her hands roam across my shoulders and back. My jeans grow tighter, and I reach down and take off Ava's. She lifts easily as I slide them down her legs. She's flushed, the rise and fall of her chest rapid, and all I want is her.

CHAPTER FIFTEEN

AVA

T HE AIR HAS LODGED itself in my throat. Connor is staring down at me, and everywhere his eyes touch, I burn. He stands now and removes his jeans and boxers, and my face lights up. I've seen men naked before, just none like Connor. My heart slams against my chest as he moves back up toward me, and I bite my lip as his fingers move under the waistband of my underwear, and he drags them painfully slow down my legs.

I want to close my eyes, but I also don't want to miss a second of this. Connor comes back up, and I spread my legs, but he pushes them together as he maneuvers himself behind me. I glance at him over my shoulder as he lifts my leg and places himself at my opening. I'm wet, I'm ready, and when he enters me, I let out a gasp. I'm slipping and falling, and I need a minute to catch myself but I can't. Brown eyes I cling to as Connor moves deeper and faster inside me. I hold on as long as I can before lying my head back down and closing my eyes. My body wants to let go; glancing at Connor one final time is what pushes me over the edge, and the world shatters around me. His release nearly undoes me again.

I'm breathless when we both lie down in a tangle of legs. I'm not sure I could survive that a second time. Connor twitches inside me, and my body betrays my thoughts. Callous skin brushes my nipples, which have already hardened, and I turn in Connor's arms. I want to watch him this time.

A banging on the front door has both of us freezing. We lie still, but as the knocking continues, Connor pulls out of me gently and places a quick kiss on my lips. Tanned bum cheeks hold my attention until they disappear into a pair of white boxers and then his jeans. That's how Connor answers the door. I lie back down until I can hear voices. After a moment, I get up and get redressed. The front door closes as I arrive into the living and kitchen area, where Connor stands topless. His head snaps up to me, and a slow grin spreads across his face. I try to cover my smile with a fist, but I can't hide it.

"That was Russell. He forgot to leave the keys for the bin area," he tells me, dangling them from his fingers. His phone is sitting on the breakfast bar in front of him, and when he glances at it, something shines in his eyes.

"Everything okay?" I ask, taking a seat at the breakfast bar.

"Yeah. My brother Darragh was at a party, but he's home now. I was just worried."

"Is he younger?" I like the idea of Connor being so protective of his brother.

"Yeah, he's one of the twins. But I'm closer to Finn. Darragh can be a bit of a handful."

"Drinking during the day was a bit of a sign," I tease. His lip tugs up, and I bite my lip. "You've got a lot of tattoos." I'm eyeing them all, and his bare skin too. He's worth looking at.

A serpent is wrapping itself around his chest and shoulders. The artwork is amazing, but there's something unsettling about the tattoo the more I study it.

"You got any?" he asks.

I join my hands and rest them on the counter. "Me and needles aren't a good match. I've always wanted one, but I'm not brave enough."

"I could go with you." Connor now takes my hand in his. "Hold your hand." His smirk has me tightening my legs together.

"I'll keep that in mind."

His eyes roam down to my mouth before flickering back up to my eyes. "We should order food." Connor takes out his phone. "Pizza?" he asks while scrolling.

"Pizza is perfect," I tell him.

He raises his lashes. "What toppings?"

"You pick." I'm hungry, but having Connor here in the kitchen, ordering food, makes me want him again. He orders mushrooms and pepperoni.

"It should be here in twenty minutes," he says as he hangs up and slides his phone into his pocket. I'm nodding as I get off the stool and walk around to Connor. He follows my every move, and my nerves kick in, but I don't stop as I reach up and touch the snake on his shoulder. His muscles clench under my touch.

"Why a snake?" I let my fingers roam across smooth tanned skin, following the serpent to his other shoulder.

"Sometimes life makes it hard to breathe, like something is tightening itself across your chest. You know? So I thought a snake was a perfect representation of that." Lines have appeared on his forehead as he frowns.

"I get that," I tell him, and I do. His hand rises and joins mine, and our fingers entwine perfectly together. Rising on tippy-toes, I kiss him softly first, opening up the invitation. I'm off the floor, and my backside rests on the counter, Connor's strong arms still wrapped around me as he deepens the kiss. My hands hold his face before roaming down his back. I'm pushing myself closer to him until I can feel all of him against me.

Kisses that he trails down my neck have me gasping when he nips me with his teeth. My nails dig into his back, and he groans before lifting me off the counter and carrying us over to the couch. Our clothes make a neat pile on the floor, my underwear the only barrier between us. Connor's fingers touch the band, and my body grows tighter, wetter at the idea of him inside me. He doesn't remove them. Instead, he slips a finger inside me, and my eyes widen. He's kneeling over me, dark brown eyes looking down at me as I push myself against his fingers. His movements grow faster, and when he dips his head down and takes one of my breasts in his mouth, I release across his fingers. I'm panting when he removes them and puts them in his mouth. His lips touch mine, and I can taste myself. Gripping his rock-hard shaft, I start to pump him.

We rotate positions until he's sitting on the couch and I'm over him, watching his face contort in pleasure. Pleasure that I'm causing, and I want him inside me. I climb onto his lap, and his eyes shoot open as I push my underwear aside and direct him inside me. Connor wraps his arms around my waist and holds me as I move up and down. I can feel that buildup inside me, and I close my eyes as I move faster. Connor's moans are making me go faster.

"Oh, fuck yeah. Faster," he says. I'm staring at him, moving as fast as my legs allow when he pours his seed inside me, his body jerking from the release. I don't come, but collapse onto his chest as we both fight for air.

We have our clothes back on when the doorbell rings. "I'll get it," I tell Connor, going for my bag, but he's already at the door taking in our pizza. The smell of the pizza has me realizing I'm starving.

We sit at the breakfast bar. Connor has put back on his gray jumper, so his skin isn't distracting me from eating. Each bite is heaven, and when I look up at Connor to find him watching me, I can't stop smiling.

"What?" I ask, and he grins. It's dark now, and the thought of him leaving has my stomach twisting. This is the part I hate, where you're not sure where you stand. After sleeping together, it changes everything.

"You're beautiful."

My smile grows until it's almost painful, and I'm covering my mouth now. "Thank you," I tell him, and he picks up a piece of pizza and starts to eat again.

"Will you stay tonight?" There, I said it.

He nods. "That was my plan."

I laugh. "What if I didn't ask you?"

"I would follow you to bed and climb in."

A laugh bursts from my lips at the image of Connor following me to bed.

We sit for a while longer and chat, but after all that happened today, I'm ready for bed. Connor tidies and locks up before we make our way to the bedroom. It feels weird to have him here. But a nice weird. I'm going through my bags, looking for my night clothes while Connor strips down. I forgot he has nothing with him. His leg muscles bunch together as he pulls his jeans down. When his shirt is pulled over his head, I have a full, clear view of his back. A large cross dominates most of the space.

"Didn't take you for a religious kind of guy," I say and realize I've put on bottoms from a different pajama set than my top. Connor is way too distracting. But they'll do. Climbing into bed, I tell my heart to relax. It's more intimate to intentionally go to bed with someone just to sleep than to have sex.

"I like to think that if we don't get punished in this life for our wrongdoings, we get punished in the next." He climbs in now and faces me.

"So you think there is more than this?" I ask as he takes my hand in his and twines our fingers together.

"I like to think so."

"So do I. I hope it's the land of milk of honey," I tell him, and he grins.

"I'm not sure about the milk and honey."

I smile into his handsome face. A final warm kiss is brushed across my lips before he turns off the overhead lights. The darkness is nice as I move closer to Connor. His scent surrounds me, along with his arms, as I fall asleep.

CHAPTER SIXTEEN

CONNOR

WAKING UP THIS MORNING to Ava in my arms is torture. She still sleeps as I stare down at her. I'm falling for this girl, and if she finds out why I'm here, it would destroy what we have.

My phone dings, and I know it's Shane or Finn wondering where I am. After getting dressed, I sit on a chair in the corner and wait until Ava wakes up. As antsy as I am to get home, she deserves to sleep. Her arms stretch over her head, and I can't stop the smile that grows on my face. When her eyes land on me, they widen slightly.

"Good morning." Her expression is shock before her cheeks turn a shade of pink. She sits up, running her hands through her hair.

"Morning." I move to the bed, and when I sit down, she gazes up at me with a sleepy look that has me brushing a kiss to her lips.

"I have to go," I tell her, and she nods but kisses me back.

"Will I see you later?"

I brush another kiss against her lips. "I should be able to get back this evening." I hope I can anyway. I don't linger much longer, or I won't leave at all.

***

I'm just in the back door when Shane starts. "Where were you? Why can't you answer your phone?"

I don't answer him. Instead, I give Mary a gentle kiss on the cheek, and I get a smile for it.

"Some toast?" she asks, and I give her another kiss.

"You're the best, Mary," I say. Shane snorts, and I sit down across from him. "I was busy," I tell him and can see a muscle clench in his jaw.

"Doing what, Connor? Your job, I hope."

I lean in close to him. "What do you want?" I'm not in the mood for Shane. His condescending ways aren't going to fly with me.

Mary puts a cup of tea and toast in front of me. Shane's staring at her.

"Thanks, Mary," I tell her. She pats my shoulder and leaves the kitchen.

"Why have you got to be such a moody fucker to Mary? If I was her, I would poison your tea."

"That's why I make my own," Shane informs me. "I spoke to Brian, and he swore blind that Harry doesn't work for him. He had no idea what I was talking about."

"Well, then it must be true." My words have Shane slamming his fist against the table.

"What's going on?" Una speaks from the door, and Shane's face transforms. A smile is forced, and he unclenches his fist.

"Nothing. How did you sleep?" he asks her sweetly as she pulls out a chair beside me.

"I slept well." Her cheeks are red as she holds a coffee cup tightly in her hands.

"You smell good. What perfume are you wearing?" I lean into Una and sniff, and she laughs before taking a drink of coffee.

"I'm not wearing perfume," she tells me, and I let surprise flitter across my face.

"Really? You need to bottle that up and sell it. You could call it Una." She's laughing, as I intended, and I don't have to look up at Shane to know his blood is boiling over.

"So where did you sleep last night?" Una raises an eyebrow.

"Yes, Connor. We would all like to know," Shane says.

I don't look at Shane. "A mates," I tell Una, and she narrows her eyes.

"Boy or a girl?"

"What do you think?" I smirk, and she smiles. Now I flicker a glance at Shane. He's ready to come out of his chair. Picking up my cup, I take a long drink.

"You okay?" I ask him. "You look a little green." His chair scrapes the floor as he stands.

"I'm fine," he informs me, trying to look calm.

"Look who's home," Darragh shouts as he arrives in the kitchen, pointing to himself. He slaps me on the back. "Sorry about being a dick yesterday," he adds before sitting up on the table beside Una.

"Me too. So all good?" I ask, not sure what to say with Una sitting here, but she's munching away at her breakfast. Finn sits down opposite me with a bowl of cereal. Shane still lingers in the kitchen. I can feel him staring at my back. When I glance over my shoulder, he's watching me.

"Yeah, charges were dropped. They had nothing on me."

I take a quick look at Una again, and she doesn't seem effected at all by what he's saying.

"So that's it?" I ask.

He nods. "Yep. Yep. I am a frrreeee man." Finn rolls his eyes at Darragh's back.

"Darragh, can you not sit on the table?" Una says. "Your ass is, like, right beside my breakfast." Darragh slides off at Una's request and pulls out a chair across from her.

"I just like being beside you, sweetheart," he tells her, and I want to look at Shane.

Una doesn't respond.

"So I was wondering if it would suit you to meet Siobhan today for lunch," Finn asks me. Shane exhales loudly enough that Una looks at him. I don't know what passes between them, but he stays silent as Finn continues. "I would really like if you met her."

"Yeah, sure. I want to see who stole my brother's heart," I declare, and he grins. "Can't wait until you find someone. You won't be teasing me then."

"Maybe he already has." Shane talks as he makes his way back to the table. "Connor never arrived home last night."

"Who were you tipping?" Darragh asks, and I don't answer him.

"I was with a mate," I say, and Shane snorts.

"So you keep saying."

My eyes snap to his, and I hold his stare. I want to say that I was with Ava, but that would go down like a ton of bricks.

Shane turns his smart mouth to Finn. "You have to bring Darragh with you. Remember our agreement?"

Finn stiffens, and when he glares at Shane, I wait for an explosion. "He's not coming to meet Siobhan. She fucking hates him."

Darragh holds his hand over his heart. "She wounds me with her words."

"Then you're not going." Shane gives a final note that I don't like.

"Don't be a dick, Shane. Darragh can take care of himself. If you're that worried, why don't you stay with him?"

Everyone seems to be holding their breaths. Una stiffens beside me, but I don't give a crap.

"Shane, I'll stay with him." Una's voice carries a note of pleading.

"No, I don't want you around him. You know that."

"Jeez, everyone seems to really hate Darragh." Darragh doesn't sound hurt at all.

"Darragh, I don't hate you." Una rests her hand on his, and I'm waiting for Shane to flip the table. It's almost comical, only I don't like Shane's attitude toward Finn.

"That's settled," I tell Shane as I get up. No one speaks as I put my cup in the sink. I need a shower and fresh clothes. I leave the kitchen, Darragh on my heels.

"So I was wondering about the job we started but didn't finish." He waggles his eyebrows as he follows me into my bedroom.

"Don't you think you're in enough trouble?" I ask while pulling off my boots.

"Nah, that case was swallowed up into a black hole."

"I don't get it. They had your fingerprints in the woman's bedroom. How did that disappear?"

Darragh smirks as he takes a cigarette from behind his ear.

"Don't light that up in my room," I warn him, and he pushes it back behind his ear.

"So turns out Siobhan's aunty was the town's bike. She was doing a few young lads, mostly farmers in the area. So they didn't just find my fingerprints but others too." He bounces down on my bed as I remove my jumper.

"So I took one for the team. Said I was banging her." He shivers, and I bark a quick laugh at him.

"You're not right in the head," I tell him, getting up and slipping my phone out of my jeans before removing them.

"So am I back in?"

"Yeah, sure." He whoops.

"Now get out of my room." I enter the bathroom and turn on the shower.

"You're the best, Connor," Darragh shouts before closing my bedroom door.

***

I meet Siobhan in a small bistro in Kingscourt. I can see her and Finn through the large front windows. They look happy. I'm approaching the table when she looks up at me. Her brown eyes, sallow skin, and long dark hair make her look foreign.

"Siobhan?" I ask, and she smiles, flashing me a set of white teeth. She half rises and takes my outstretched hand.

"So great to meet you." She seems genuinely happy, and Finn is grinning as I sit down. Guilt churns in my stomach at seeing him happy with me here. He must have been so angry when I left.

"You too. Finn here won't shut up about you."

A small laugh bubbles up her throat, and she smiles across at Finn. "All good, I hope?"

"Every single word was praising you." She smiles softly again. She's easy to chat with, and we reminisce and laugh a lot. It makes me remember how much I missed Finn and how I don't think I can walk away and leave him behind again. And now it isn't just Finn I would be leaving but Ava too. That's becoming less of an option as each day moves by.

When Siobhan goes to bathroom, I know what Finn will ask. "So, what do you think?" He's looking for approval.

"Of what?" I get a smack on the arm for that, and I grin. "She's exactly what I thought she would be. You did good." His smile is wide now as he plays with the sugar sachets on the table.

"I'm going to ask her to marry me."

"That's a big commitment." That would be the first O'Reagan wedding.

"Yeah, I want her forever." His words are sincere, and it makes my mind go to Ava.

"You've turned into quite the sap," I tell him to lighten the mood, and he shrugs.

"What can I say?" His eyes flicker up, and Siobhan sits down.

"So what about you, Connor? Have you got a girlfriend?" Her innocent question doesn't feel so innocent to me.

"No, I can't seem to find one that will stay."

She giggles. "I don't believe that for a second." She's sweet, and I'm happy for Finn. Out of all of us, he deserves a happily ever after. We stay for a while longer before Siobhan has to get ready for work.

"It was a pleasure meeting you." I give both her cheeks a kiss and wink at Finn. But he isn't like Shane. He looks happy with my affection toward Siobhan. Finn goes back with Siobhan, and

I drive my car back to the house. When I arrive, I pull my phone out and text Ava.

How is your day?

I sit in the car and wait for Ava to text back; it doesn't take her long.

Here with Nan. She's so happy you stayed last night. So am I. x Will I see you tonight?

Ah, shit. I should have checked to see if she needed to be dropped off anywhere.

How did you get there? Tell Nan I said hi. I'll be there tonight. X

Looking up, I see Shane leaning against the garage door. He just isn't going to give me a break today.

I read Ava's message before getting out.

Taxi. Nan said hi back. LOL Okay I will have food ready. What time?

"You can't be interfering in how we run things here," Shane bites out.

I slam the car door. "I'm not one of your lackeys, Shane." I move past him, and he pushes me back into the garage. I clench my fists.

"Don't touch me again," I warn him, and he raises both eyebrows.

"Darragh is a loose cannon. Finn is the only one who can keep him in line."

"I. Don't. Care." I say each word clearly. "I won't sit here as you dictate where we can and can't go."

Shane nods. "Like how you crossed into the north when you shouldn't have."

My heart stills, but I remember to breath and not let my facial expression show anything. "You're as bad as Liam. I was in Monaghan. That's hardly the fucking north."

"Belfast. Father's informant told us."

I nod. "Well, he's not doing a very good job is he? And have you actually met him?" I fold my arms across my chest. "I didn't think so, Shane. Are we done?"

"You seem to forget that I have eyes everywhere. So I do hope you're sleeping with Ava to gain information for me." His smirk has me taking a step back before I wipe it off his face.

"She knows nothing."

"Is that why she was seen at the Gardaí station?"

Bastard has eyes everywhere.

"I don't get you, Shane. Why put me on the job if you have others on it?"

"Because I don't trust you."

"Then ask one of your other brothers to do it."

He shifts and looks away before remembering himself and relaxing, but the tell was there. He can't go to them. Why, I'm not sure. "I will."

His lie has me snorting at him. "So my job here is done?" I ask, hoping to catch him, but I don't like his response at all.

"Yeah, consider your job done." He leaves the garage, and his words unsettle me. He has someone watching Ava. I just pray it isn't Brian. I shoot off another text to Ava.

I should be there around eight. If you need me for anything, just ring. X

I return to the house feeling unsettled. I didn't really think Shane would dismiss me like that. That could mean I read this situation completely wrong, or he's going to take care of it himself. The thoughts of him putting his hands near Ava has me stiffening. Panic swirls viciously inside my stomach, and when I find him in the kitchen alone, I can't help my next words. They're stupid and reckless, but I need to protect Ava. Right now, there seems to be only one thing that Shane cares about more than himself.

He looks up immediately when I step into the kitchen. I don't know what he sees in my eyes, but he's standing now.

"If you touch Ava, and I mean one hair on her head, I will hurt Una." The lie sounds convincing with how my body coils and tightens at the idea of him hurting Ava.

His response is unexpected. He charges me. I'm not ready and find myself on my back. His fists hit my face hard and fast, and

I flip him on one of his pauses. I don't hesitate but make each punch heavy and fast. He gains the upper hand again as he pushes my head into the floor, his knee connecting with my back and knocking the air from my lungs.

If I don't get out of this position, he'll win. I snap my head back, connecting with his face. I'm released and standing. Shane's up too as blood sprays from his nose and makes a pathway down his shirt. Liquid drips from my ears, and when I brush my fingertips to my ear, my fingers come away slick with blood.

"That one's for free," I tell him, and he charges again, only this time I'm ready. The uppercut connects with his chin, and Shane's head snaps back as he stumbles and hits the floor. That punch has taken many men down, but Shane is getting back up.

"You want some more?" I'm egging him on when Liam arrives.

"That's enough," he warns us, and Shane seems to loosen, but he hasn't taken his eyes off me. I drop my fists.

"Yeah, I'll let you walk away this time," I tell Shane, and his temper snaps again as he moves toward me. I'm ready, but Liam wraps an arm around Shane's chest.

"Some battles you just can't win," he tells Shane, and I smirk.

"You hear that? Even Liam thinks you're weak." I watch a vein bulge along his neck.

"No, Connor, you're wrong. Shane will outmaneuver you any day. He just won't use his fists, while fists is all you have. That will fade with time, and then so will you."

"Fuck you," I tell Liam and leave the room. I want to hurt someone. His words shadow my thoughts now, and I know he will outmaneuver me when it comes to Ava. Because this is what Shane is good at.

CHAPTER SEVENTEEN

AVA

N AN LOOKS SO MUCH brighter today, and she's been a ray of sunshine since I told her about Connor spending the night and coming over again tonight.

"You be careful, birdy. That one has the armor to break hearts," she warns me, and I know she's right. I'm already falling hard for Connor. Any more time with him, and I'll be in so deep that I won't be able to get back out.

"But who am I kidding? That boy is here to stay. Just look at you, birdy. A heart of gold."

I squeeze Nan's hand. "I really like him," I confess.

"Don't I know. It's written all over your face. You're in love."

My eyes widen. "I don't think it's love, but..." It's pretty close. "Anyway, I have to get to work. I'm on a short shift, only three to seven."

"Okay, sweetheart. Now don't be coming back up here tomorrow. Take the day off, and I'll see you when you have time."

I kiss her cheek and ignore her. "I'll see you again in the morning," I tell her, and she purses her lips together trying to appear all annoyed.

"See you, birdy, and love you."

"Love you too," I tell her, and I leave the hospital ward and make my way down to the taxi rank.

I get to work twenty minutes later. I'm early, but I head on in and am surprised to find the bar and lounge empty. Normally, Paul and his friends would be here, but the place is deserted.

"Hello?" I call out as I stuff my bag and jacket under the desk.

I scream as Patrick seems to materialize at the other side of the bar. "Jesus, Patrick, I didn't see you." I'm half laughing as I clutch my heart.

"Ah, sorry, Ava. I didn't mean to scare you."

I'm waving off his apology. "Hope everything was alright the other day. I was worried."

Patrick looks away with guilt shadowing his eyes. I try to think and remember now how I left work, running out the door like the hounds of hell were on my heels.

"I forgot. Yeah, everything was fine. Don't be worrying." Now I understand his guilt. He had, after all, stood there without intervening. Patrick scratches his jaw, dark circles under his eyes, makes me want to take away his guilt. He has enough on his plate, and going up against Brian isn't exactly an option.

"Everything is fine, Patrick," I reassure him again, and this time when he glances up, he nods, desperate to believe me. "I better get to work before the boss catches me slacking," I tell him, and he smiles a little.

All through my shift, I can only think of one thing: Connor. He consumes my every thought. Paul and his friends arrive and even ask me what I'm smiling about.

"Mind your own business," I answer, but I can't stop the stupid smile that keeps creeping across my face.

I start to polish all the glasses that are never used but are mostly decoration above the bar. The dust has me sneezing, and I make a mental note not to let it get into this kind of state again.

"Ava." It's Paul's voice that has me looking down, but my eyes snap to Brian, who stands beside him.

My heart immediately starts to slam against my chest. I drop the cloth and get down off the bar. "I went to your place last night, but you weren't there. Where were you?" His blue eyes are ablaze with anger.

"You're barred!" My voice carries across the bar, but the anger I feel right now isn't containable. He might have put his hands on me, but not my nan. She raised me, loved me, protected me, and I brought him to her door.

"Get out!" My shouts make him flinch, and it gives me a sense of power. I can feel Patrick standing behind me.

"You heard her. You're barred." At first, Patrick's words give me a confidence I haven't had in a while, until Brian starts to laugh.

"Patrick, get your dumb ass in the back and close your little door," Brian says. And like that, I'm reminded of the power that Brian holds over people. Patrick doesn't move, and Brian's eyes flash with violence. I don't want to see Patrick hurt, and I bow my head, ready to give in.

"I think you should leave," Paul says. Him and his friends are holding pool sticks, all ready for action. If you ignore the slight tremble in Paul's voice, or how his friends' hands shake, you would think they could win this.

"What are you serving today, Ava? Courage? Because if everyone doesn't take a step back from me, I'm really going to lose it. You want that, Ava? You want more people hurt because of you?" Brian grips the bar like it's my neck. This is all going to end badly.

"Paul, please, it's fine. I'm fine." They move away, and they all wear a look of relief. My eyes dim, but Brian's seem to shine with victory. Patrick doesn't leave, and I don't ask him to.

"What do you want?" I grit my teeth.

"I want you to tell me where you were last night."

"At home."

His fist slams into the bar counter. "Stop lying. I checked."

"What, you can see through my door?"

"No, Ava. I got a key off Sean. Some of your clothes were gone."

I want to throw up on the counter. He was in my apartment, with my stuff, and as for Sean giving out my key without permission, he really is the worst landlord ever.

"I stayed at a hotel."

"Which one?"

"Jesus, Brian, can't you just leave me alone?" The whine in my voice comes through.

"You lied to me, Ava. You're still lying to me."

"Brian, maybe you should go." Patrick speaks behind me. The sound is odd.

"Maybe you should shut your mouth before I close it permanently." His threat has Patrick tutting, but silence falls. Now I pray for customers, but no one arrives.

"Patrick, can I take a break?" I ask, still looking at Brian.

"Yeah, take whatever time you need."

I don't turn to Patrick as I move up the bar and watch Brian follow me. I grab my bag and coat and try to make my way outside; it will be safer if I'm surrounded by lots of people. But Brian blocks the door.

"You're testing my patience, Ava." He takes a step toward me, and I take one back.

"I just want to be left alone," I tell him and soften my voice.

"Please, Brian, just let me go." My words were meant to make him remember what we had, but they don't. Instead, he throws his head back and starts laughing.

"That's not going to happen, sweetheart."

"What do you want from me?" I'm shouting again, but I can't keep doing this.

"You. I want you." He grips my arms and bile rises up my throat.

"I don't want you," I whisper to him, knowing that will bring out his anger.

"You're such a dumb tramp." His words are as effective as a slap to the face. I step away from him and don't respond. "I'm the only fucking reason you're alive." He runs his hands through his hair.

I have no idea what that means, but Brian has a vision of himself as a God. "I want to leave. Move." My throat burns, but I need to get away from him now. His hands grip my shoulders again, his fingers digging in.

"Where the fuck were you last night?" His anger is vibrating up my arms.

"With Connor." I know I shouldn't say it, but I want to see the hurt on his face, and the moment I do, I regret it.

His slap knocks me to the floor. "You're such a fucking slut, Ava."

I'm staring at gray tiles, telling my lungs to take in oxygen, telling myself that this can't happen again. I'm picturing my nan, so small in the hospital, and thinking how he put his hands on her. I'm up, and when my hand connects with his face, the sound is so satisfying. I get two slaps in before he gets over the shock. He grips my wrists, and the pain runs up my arms. I try to knee him in the balls, but he moves his leg.

"You're going to regret that," he tells me.

"The only thing I regret is setting eyes on you. You make me sick."

He pushes me against the bar, and my back erupts in pain. Everything seems to happen so fast. I glimpse Patrick behind him, a heavy crystal ashtray in his hand, and it comes down on Brian's head. His eyes widen, and he stares at me in confusion before releasing me as he falls to the floor.

"Go, Ava. You need to leave now."

I'm struggling to breathe, but I'm nodding, picking up my bag that must have fallen in the struggle.

I'm out the door. The fresh air makes me question whether that just happened. Tears burn my eyes as I run down the street while glancing back over my shoulder. My eyes scan the few people, but none of them are Brian. *Deep breaths*, I tell myself while trying to calm my erratic heartbeat. My face burns, and with shaky hands, I touch it. He didn't break the skin this time.

Patrick won't just walk away from hitting Brian over the head. I slow my pace and stop in a doorway. The step is cold under me; my legs are unable to carry me any further. My hand trembles as I push hair behind my ear. A couple walks past me and eyes me suspiciously. I wonder if they would stop if I were to ask them for help. I'm scrolling through my phone, trying to calm myself as I search for Connor's number. Reality is, he will try to pick a fight with Brian and end up hurt too. I want to scream in frustration.

"Ava." The roar of my name has me frozen on the step. Brian was always possessive, but this is psychotic. Should I run to the Gardaí station? They might not let me press charges, but surely they couldn't let him beat me. I'm up now and running around by the credit union. When he shouts my name again, I know he sees me. It's all uphill now, and he's gaining on me. Blood soaks his shirt, but I can't see where from. It must be the back of his head. A part of me wants to stop running and plead with him not to do this, but I don't think he could be reasoned with in this state.

"Ava, I just want to talk." His words are meant to calm me, but they drive a panic through my system that makes me run faster.

I'm weaving between traffic, my panic escalating. A black Mercedes stops in front of me, and I recognize the taxi man. I'm in the passenger seat looking over my shoulder. "Headfort Demesne. Please. Quickly." The taxi man doesn't ask questions, and I watch Brian grow smaller in the mirror.

CHAPTER EIGHTEEN

CONNOR

MY EAR IS STILL bleeding, and I wipe blood away using my sleeve. I'm in the hall when Mary opens the door. Two detectives are in the doorway, showing Mary their badges. She turns to me and so do the two men.

"Liam," I call over my shoulder. He appears beside me. "You got visitors," I tell him. He fixes his tie and walks toward Mary. His confidence is something to be admired. I don't go into my room. My ear is killing me. I move closer to make sure I don't miss a beat. The one on the right with a shaky beard eyes me, and I give him a nod. His attention returns to Liam.

"What can I do for you gentlemen?" Liam places a hand on Mary's shoulder, dismissing her, and she scurries past me and into the kitchen. A grin spreads across my face at her large inhale. Shane must still be in the kitchen, his face a bloody mess.

A piece of paper is passed to Liam. He accepts but doesn't look at it. "What is this?" he asks.

"A warrant to search land that's registered in Michael O'Reagan's name."

Liam hands them back their warrant, and they glance at one another. "I trust you. Let us know when you're done. Anything else I can help you gentlemen with today?" They look as confused as I feel.

The one with the beard takes the warrant and places it in the pocket of his jacket. "That's all today."

Once Liam has the door closed, something changes in his posture, and he moves quickly back toward the kitchen. So everything isn't okay. I follow him into the kitchen.

"Mary, the rest of the day is yours," Liam tells her. Mary doesn't miss a beat as she moves past us, grabbing her jacket and going out the back door. Shane stands taller when I walk into the kitchen.

"Now's not the time. We just had two detectives at the door. They have a warrant to search the bog."

Liam's words have Shane's anger toward me deflating. "I've moved all the bodies," he tells Liam while getting ice out of the fridge. After wrapping ice cubes in a towel, he holds it to his face. My ear is on fire. I do the same, wrapping some ice cubes in a towel and holding it to my ear.

"All the bodies? I thought it was just the old woman."

"So you found the girl?" Liam says to Shane. No one answers me, but now that makes two.

"You lied to me. You told me you rang it in," Shane says back through gritted teeth.

"How long have you known?" Liam sounds almost impressed.

Shane looks away. "I found the body a while later."

"And dare I ask what you were doing up there?" Liam questions, and the answer is clear—burying a body. That makes three.

"Where are they all now?" I ask, and finally Shane looks at me.

"Loch Leigh Mountain."

On our back door. But they would be well hidden, and we owned land at the base of it.

"You did that all yourself?" Liam questions.

"Yes, Liam." Shane's anger is under the surface, ready to break through. I don't understand what Liam is saying that is riling him up so much. But the mention of the girl's body has the tension building in the room.

"So we have nothing to worry about?" Liam is like a dog with a bone. I remove the cloth from my ear. Blood soaks the towel, and I want to punch Shane again.

"I made sure everything was removed. Unless you buried more people and forgot to mention it?"

"No, you seem to have found them all. I'll inform Darragh and Finn." Liam leaves the room, and I'm alone with Shane.

"I think you busted my eardrum," I tell him and he glares at me.

"Good." He moves past me but pauses at my shoulder. "Get ready. We better all go down to the bog and intimidate the fuckers."

"You think that's wise?" I ask his retreating back.

"Yes, Connor, I do."

I change my shirt and hang out in the garage as I wait for the others. My phone is in my pocket on silent, but I check it before Finn arrives into the garage. Nothing from Ava. I slide it into my pocket and get into the car while Finn jumps into the passenger seat.

"This is so fucked up. This is beside were Siobhan lives." He scratches his brow as he stares out the window. "I was the one that convinced her to sell us the land." Now he faces me. "I wish I never had."

I get what he is saying. I wish I had never approached Ava under false pretenses, because now I have no idea how all this ends.

"Yeah, it seems a mess," I tell him as Darragh comes out into the garage. His eyes meet mine, and he rubs his hands together.

"You better wipe that smile off your face," Finn barks at Darragh as he climbs into the back. He's like a child ready to go on a road trip. Darragh lights up, and I let him smoke. I reverse out as Shane and Liam get into separate vehicles.

"I think it's dumb, us going down there." Darragh blows smoke in between the seats.

"I think it's dumb that you killed Siobhan's aunt." Finn swings around in the seat and faces Darragh.

"Yeah, I'm sorry, man," Darragh replies. I can't see him, but I can picture him shrugging.

"What about the girl?" I ask and move the rearview mirror so I can see him. Guilt is there across his face.

"She was a pro." He shrugs now like I pictured he had before.

"You killed someone else?" Finn yells. I tap him on the shoulder to try to get him to calm down and sit back down. He turns around in his seat.

"Jesus. I was banging her, and she was dead—I think, a junkie. So yeah, she's there too."

"Anyone else?" Finn asks, but he's growing paler by the second.

"I don't know."

We grow silent as we pull up beside the land. Shane's and Liam's vehicles pull up across the road beside the detective's cars and a forensic van. Neither Liam nor Shane get out of their vehicles, so we sit in mine as Darragh lights up another cigarette. Finn rolls down his window, and I glance at Darragh in the mirror. He grins as he blows smoke out of the side of his mouth and toward Finn.

The moment Shane steps out of his car, I grin. He has cleaned all the blood away, but his face is red, bruised, and swollen. I feel satisfied.

"You sure did a number on him," Darragh says, blowing smoke too close to my face.

"I'll do a number on you if you don't blow that smoke somewhere else." That somewhere else becomes Finn, who swings around and faces Darragh.

"Come on. Lets go," I tell them, getting out before they kill each other. I don't remember them ever fighting this much.

Liam steps out wearing a full-length trench coat. He fits the criminal mastermind bill to a tee. I want to tell him to tone it down, but it's Liam.

"What I don't understand is how they know we had land here and why they decided to check. You said all charges were dropped against Darragh." Shane questions Liam.

"Finding out we own the land wouldn't be hard, and with Darragh's connection to the aunt and Finn to Siobhan, they would piece it together. Why they're searching is the part I want to know." Liam moves forward, and we all find ourselves falling into place beside him.

No one stops us as we move across the land to where a digger is tearing up the ground.

"They're digging in the right place," Shane tells Liam. Someone squealed. The two detectives that were at the door turn to see us coming, and the one with the beard approaches us.

"You can't be here right now." His eyes flicker across all of us, but he addresses Liam.

"You got your men and equipment here fast," Liam counteracts.

"They were on standby. You need to leave, Mr. O'Reagan."

Darragh snorts, but the detective holds Liam's stare.

"David, isn't it?" Liam asks. The detective stands a little straighter. "David O'Hara?" Liam says his name slowly, and David's jaw tightens.

"My name is no concern to you." He doesn't sound so sure now.

The digger stops digging. "We got something." The man on the digger jumps down and fixes a cap on his head before going over to the hole.

David smirks at us like we're all going down. The forensics team, all in white suits, moves in. I want to see what's in the hole. One of them glances at David.

"Detective," he calls, and David gives us all a warning look. "None of you move." He turns and goes over to the men.

"What could be there?" Liam asks, and when I glance at Shane, he's grinning.

"I buried livestock around the place."

I'm grinning now as they pull out the carcass of a cow.

"Finn." We all turn as a female voice comes from behind us. It's Siobhan. Her red puffy eyes and folded arms have us all feeling a bit sorry for Finn.

He's beside her, shaking his head. "What are you doing here?"

"I heard they're digging here, looking for a body. Is that true?" Her voice rises, and Shane clenches his hands.

"It's all a mistake, Siobhan." He doesn't sound convincing. Siobhan glances up at me, and I nod, but she refocuses on Finn.

"You never told me that Darragh was brought in for questioning about my aunt."

Oh, Christ. I didn't pity him for one moment.

"He needs to get rid of her," Liam tells Shane, who turns to do that, and I step in his way.

"Leave him alone. Just give him a minute." We stare at each other. I don't want to fight, but that would make everything worse for Finn.

"The charges were dropped, Siobhan," Finn says. "Darragh is an asshole."

Darragh snorts at that. "Everyone loves calling me names," he mumbles under his breath.

"But he is no killer." This time, I believe Finn.

David is making his way back, and Liam is right. Siobhan shouldn't be here for this.

"Hi." I approach them with hands in my pockets. "They are nearly finished, but they want everyone off the land." I give an apologetic shrug. "Maybe you should take Siobhan home," I suggest.

"Yeah, you're right." Finn wraps an arm around Siobhan, and she leans into him. "I'll catch you later." Finn leaves.

"See, you don't have to be a dick to get the job done," I tell Shane.

"Okay, you all need to leave now." David doesn't meet anyone's eye, embarrassed that he didn't find a body.

"Tell your wife I said hi," Darragh says while blowing smoke toward David. Sometimes, I don't get him. Why does he antagonize the Gardaí?

"Get off this land." His shoulders tense as he approaches Darragh.

Darragh flicks his cigarette on the ground. "I was leaving anyway."

"We can use that as evidence." David points to the cigarette butt, and Darragh laughs.

"If you had my sperm inside a woman, you dumb cunts still couldn't solve the case."

That is how you get yourself arrested.

Liam shakes his head as Darragh is put in cuffs and escorted off the land by a female Gardaí he gives abuse to.

"Now, I suggest you leave before I arrest you all." David's final warning has me turning. I reach my car as the one Gardaí pulls off with Darragh in the back seat, grinning like he's off to a party.

Shane waves me over as he climbs into Liam's Jeep. The Jeep is still warm as I climb into the back.

"Someone reported us. They're digging in the exact same spot where the bodies were." Liam glances at me in the rearview mirror.

"I've never stood on that land, so don't look at me."

"I'm not, Connor. I just want you to question Darragh and find out if he did."

"Ask him yourself." I reach for the handle, ready to get out, but the door won't open. "A child lock. You think that will keep me in?" I ask Liam.

"We are having a civilized conversation. Everything doesn't have to resort to violence."

I flick the door handle roughly a few times to get a reaction out of Liam, but I don't succeed.

"Finn?" Liam questions, looking at Shane.

"No, he's too loyal, and he wouldn't drop himself into the middle of a murder investigation. Especially now, with Siobhan." Shane's logic is correct. If I put my money on anyone, it would be Darragh.

"That leaves us with Darragh." Liam looks at me again in the review mirror.

"Why don't I go bail him out and ask him," I suggest. The locks pop, and I open my door.

"They took him to Nobber Gardaí station." I don't ask Liam how he knows, but I run across the road and get into my car. The smell of smoke has me rolling down the window as I head for Nobber.

***

"I'm here to bail out Darragh O'Reagan."

The female Gardaí stares at me, her eyes dead as she focuses on her screen and types away. They have one holding cell here. I know because I sat in it many times. Mostly for fighting.

I glance around at the small reception area as my phone vibrates. As I'm reaching for it, my thoughts go to Ava.

Mark McGuiness is home alone now.

The message is from Neill, and the name is one of the guys that beat him up.

"I knew you would come rescue me."

I turn as Darragh is brought out by the bangharda. He's winking at her as she removes the cuffs. "Maybe when you're off duty, we could get a drink." She has a face that would sour milk as she pushes Darragh toward the door.

I grin, and he holds his hands over his heart. "Shot down again," he tells me as we leave the station.

"You need to control your mouth," I inform him, and he lights up a cigarette as he climbs into the car.

"I'm only having a laugh. Everyone is so uptight."

No traffic is coming, and I pull out onto the road. "So I've been tasked with asking you if you told anyone where the bodies were buried."

"They're dumb fucks," Darragh says, and I flicker a quick glance at him. "Why would I tell anyone? I don't think this face would fare well in prison. I would be a piece of meat."

I'm grinning at him. "Yeah, I thought as much, but I had to ask."

"I don't mind that everyone thinks I'm that much of a fuckup." His words are said with a smile, but something darker lingers in them.

"How about we blow off some steam?"

He's sitting up in the car now, his head bobbling. "What you got in mind? Women? Drinks?" He's working himself up.

"More like hurting someone," I say.

"I'm down with that."

CHAPTER NINETEEN

CONNOR

I HAVE EVERYTHING IN the boot of the car, so we don't need to swing by home. My phone starts to ring. It's Liam, but I hit silent. Darragh smirks. "You'll pay for that later."

"What can he do?" I ask Darragh. Their fear of Liam is nearly unjustified. I never remember him putting his hand on any of us. He never raises his voice. I know I've always felt an element of respect toward him but not fear. Yet, even Shane wouldn't disobey Liam.

"Whatever he wants." Darragh's tone is low as he faces the window.

"Like what?"

"I don't know, man. Whatever. He's just scary." His lie is delivered with a smirk.

I want to dig further, but we're coming up on Mark's house. His house is only three miles outside of Kells. I pull into an opening a few houses down. Cattle roam the fields. It's drizzling, so I hope that keeps any walkers inside.

"We'll leave the car here," I tell Darragh and get everything we need from the boot of the car. I hand him the balaclava and his bat, and he strokes her.

"Now you got to follow my lead," I tell Darragh while closing the trunk. "No killing animals at all."

He closes his eyes slightly. "Fine."

It's always a mistake to bring Darragh on a job, but he's easy to work with. We hop the side wall. Electric gates rise high into the air, but the walls on either side are low, defeating the purpose. We both move quietly along the side of the house. My eyes move quickly, checking the corner of the house for cameras, but apart from the gates, the house is easy to get into.

The double doors off the patio are unlocked, and I nod at Darragh. We pull the balaclavas over our faces as I push open the door and wait a beat before entering. Mark is messy; bundles of clothes are stacked on the table. Not just male but also female, and a pile of small children's clothing sits right in the center. Dishes are stacked up in the sink, and leftovers still sit in open takeout containers.

We move into the hall. Straight ahead are several doors, and there's one to my left. I point for Darragh to check it as I move down the hall. The first room is a utility room that stinks of rubbish that spills over the side of a bin. The next room is a bedroom. I'm not sure if it's for a male or female—everything is cream.

"You enjoying yourself?" Darragh's voice sounds loud in the silence, and another muffled voice sounds next.

"What the fuck?" I make my way toward the voices.

The room that Darragh checked is a sitting room. The rich red rug under my feet is soft, and the cream leather sofas look new. Mark has his dick in his hand.

"Nothing worse than being caught with your trousers down, huh?" Darragh laughs at him while pointing the bat at his head. I hold up my hand in warning.

Mark tucks his dick back into his pants and sits up. His white vest top showcases that both arms are covered in tats. A diamond earing flashes in the light.

"I'm going to make this really simple," I say. "We're the guys that got your friend David." His face pales a little, and I'm glad my message got around. "So you know why we're here, then."

He nods but holds up his hands. "Look, we just do the jobs we get paid to do. That's it. It's not personal. It's just a job."

I push a cushion over his face and hold him down. "His hip."

Darragh swings wide, and the crack has Mark screaming and wriggling under my hold.

"Help me hold him," I say. Darragh grabs his legs as he continues to thrash under us. "Who paid you?" I ask and lift the cushion.

"Man, you know they'll kill me."

I cover his face again, and he screams. One nod to Darragh has him swinging the bat down on his ankles. Mark's screams tear through the room, but his thrashing has lessened.

"Please stop." Drool mixes with tears as he pleads with us.

"Just tell me who paid."

He's nodding now. "Brian."

"Brian paid you to beat up Neill?" That makes no sense.

"Brian is a twisted fucker. It's possible," Darragh says while leaning on his bat.

"Look, I don't know why. All I know is he wanted him beaten pretty bad, and we told Neill it was from Brian." I believe him.

"So we're good." He's half crying, and I pat him on the head.

"Yeah, we're good." He protests as I cover his face again and let Darragh take some of his frustration out with his bat.

We leave as easily as we arrived. Neill knowing that Brian sent the men makes me question everything about him. Why didn't' he tell me?

Once we're back in the car, I check my phone. Six missed calls from Liam. I dial him back.

Liam answers the phone. "Did you manage to collect Darragh?"

"Yeah, you want to talk to him?" I ask, pulling out and onto the road.

"Did you ask?" Liam replies. I glance at Darragh. His leg is up on my dash as he stares out the window.

"Yeah, and he didn't tell anyone. Like he said, he's too good looking for prison."

Darragh snorts before lighting up another cigarette.

"Where are you now?" Liam asks.

"On our way home," I tell him. He hangs up with not even a goodbye.

"Is he always so moody?" I ask Darragh, and he grins.

****

I don't go in. I drop Darragh off before I turn the car and make my way to Ava. Why would Brian have Neill beaten up? Why would Neill lie to me about it? The security waves me on in at Headfort Demesne, and I pull up outside.

After ringing the bell four times and getting no answer, I ring Ava's phone.

"I'm at the door," I tell her the moment she answers.

"One second." She sounds strange. I can hear movement inside, and when she opens the door, her head is ducked down. Her shoulders hunch forward like they're trying to wrap themselves around her and protect her.

I close the door behind me, and she still hasn't looked up. Dread snakes its way down my spine. All I can think of is that Shane told her. Somehow she knows.

"Ava."

She looks up at me when I whisper her name. My blood turns to ice in my veins, and I'm holding her face and moving her into the light.

"Who did this?" My voice sounds calm.

"I don't know what to do anymore." Tears fall down her cheeks and make a pathway to her chin before they free fall. Her face is swollen and red, so the slap was hard, but it didn't break the skin.

"When did this happen?"

"At work."

I nod. "Let's take a look." I shrug out of my jacket and get a towel and some ice out of the freezer.

"I already iced it," she tells me, and I take a deep breath. Moving, doing something, is keeping me calm. I continue what I'm doing.

She's standing at the counter. Ava inhales deeply when I press the towel to her face. I search her face for any other marks, but it seems to be the only one.

"Are you hurt anywhere else?" I question. She looks up at me from under wet lashes.

"My back." Her lip trembles, and I focus on the material in my hand, on the counter behind Ava, on everything but her.

"Can you say something?" I look into watery green eyes and clench my jaw.

"Let me see your back." She nods as I remove the towel from her face.

Lifting her top, she turns around. "Is it bad?"

My fingers gently touch the bruised skin. "No," I lie. "Is it sore?"

"I took two painkillers. It's not so bad now."

Everything inside me is climbing, scouring, and wanting out. My arms wrap around Ava as I bury my head in her neck. I don't want to say I'm sorry. That I should have dealt with this earlier. I don't want to give her excuses. So I hold her. She turns in my arms, her eyes searching my face.

"I fought back," she tells me proudly, and I place my forehead against hers. I nod, because words have failed me. I want her to stop talking. I can't bear to hear another second of it. I want to remove the pain in her eyes.

My lips touch hers, and I wait for her to kiss me back. I won't proceed if she doesn't, but Ava kisses me back with a ferocity that I match. The kiss seems to calm the rage inside me, and I slow our pace, kissing her softly. I keep closing my eyes, but each time, my mind paints me a picture of what might have happened. Emerald green eyes stare into mine.

I'm searching her face as her breath brushes against my lips. This feeling of rage mixed with something else is unlike anything I have ever felt before.

My hand finds her, and I guide her to the bedroom. Her wide eyes and swollen lips make her look innocent. I close the door behind me and take her face in my hands, kissing her lips softly. I ignore the tightness of my jeans and the hunger to be inside her, and I focus only on her.

I move my mouth across her cheek before kissing her damaged one. I want to erase the marks that he left on her.

"Your silence is a bit frightening." Ava whispers the words against my neck.

"I'm not silent. I'm just communicating in a different way." The only way I can right now. She nods her understanding. "Raise your arms."

She does immediately, and I pull her top over her head. Reaching around her, I unclip her bra and let it move down her arms. I follow it with kisses. On my knees now, I press my lips to her flat stomach and she inhales deeply, her hands sinking into my hair.

As I rise, her hands fall to my shoulders. My tongue flickers out along her collarbone, and she inhales deeply again. Her nipples brush against my chest, and my jeans tighten further, painfully. Her hands are warm when I remove them from my shoulders and turn her around. She doesn't question me as I start at her back next and trail kisses across the bruises. Her wounds feel like my wounds. I could have stopped this. Air lodges itself in my lungs, and the snake tightens its hold.

"Connor?" Ava turns around, and I'm struggling to meet her eye. "Make love to me." Her request is spoken so gently that it feels fragile, like glass that should be wrapped in cotton wool.

I'm nodding as I remove her trousers and then her underwear. Ava stands still. She doesn't try to hide herself. She allows me to see her. My jeans fall to the floor along with my boxers, and I give Ava the same time to examine me. When her eyes travel back up to mine and her cheeks are flushed, I move us back onto the bed. My hand touches her knees, and she spreads her legs, allowing me access. She's tight and wet when I enter her, and we both exhale. My arms hold me above her as I move slowly, my eyes never leaving hers. Her hands reach out and direct my face to hers. There's a pause. It's brief. Her lips move, but no words come out before she kisses me. When her tongue moves into my mouth, my control slips, and I deepen the kiss and my thrust. She feels so good under me.

"Ah, Connor." When she calls my name, I'm moving faster, pumping harder, and I keep climbing. Her soft skin brushes mine. Her breasts bounce as I push my body harder and faster, and when she screams my name, I pour my seed inside her.

***

I feel worse after. I thought it might help the rage, but it only pushed it into the cage, and now the beast is rattling its cage.

"Connor?" Ava lies in my arms, her fingers roaming across my tattoos,like she might understand them better.

"Yeah?" I answer, placing a kiss on her forehead.

"What's your favorite color?"

"Green." I kiss her nose. "The same green as your eyes."

She narrows her eyes and smirks. "Such a charmer."

"I bet yours is brown," I tease.

"Blue. Ocean blue. I find it calming."

I store away all the little snippets she shares with me.

"I keep waiting for you to run out the door." Her confession is said with furrowed brows.

I'm up on an elbow so I can see her face fully. "Why would you say that?"

Her cheeks pinken. "Just... since you met me, I've brought so much disarray into your life."

"My life was in disarray well before you came along," I tell her.

"Like what?" She doesn't seem to believe me.

"Okay, remember my brother Darragh?" She nods. "He wasn't at a party the other day. He was being held in the Gardaí station on suspicion of murder."

She's clutching the blanket.

"He didn't," I tell her. "All charges were dropped."

Her grip loosens. "I'm so sorry you had to go through that."

I'm lying back down. "It's nothing really. But just don't ever think I'm going to run," I tell the ceiling. It's her running that's the real issue. She just doesn't know it yet.

She takes the position that I just had. Leaning over me, she kisses my shoulder. "I want to know everything about you."

No, you don't.

"What do you want to know?"

She chews her lip. "Have you had many girlfriends?"

"Yes."

Her nostril's flare, but she nods. "I've had lots of boyfriends."

Her statement does two things to me. One, I know she's saying it because she's jealous, so that makes me feel a bit taller, but I also don't like the idea of anyone else touching her.

"I don't want to know." I clench my jaw so I don't say anymore. Her soft laugh has me raising both eyebrows at her.

"It's nice when you're jealous." She's still smiling down at me when her phone rings. I'm up, moving to it.

"It's Patrick," I tell her, but her eyes are glued to the bottom part of my body.

Her hand shoots out. "Let me answer. I'd say he's worried."

I give her the phone and get dressed. The reality of what happened to her is crashing back down on me. I order a pizza again as she chats with Patrick. She's thanking him for helping her.

I give her space as she chats and wait in the living area. Ava arrives into the living area wearing a pair of tiny shorts and an oversized T-shirt, but the worry in her eyes has me forgetting her tanned legs.

"What's wrong?"

"Patrick doesn't think it's a good idea for me to go back to work."

"I agree with Patrick."

"No, Connor. Why should I lose my job because of Brian? And if I don't have a job, I don't have money, and I can't do anything."

I hold her hands in mine. "Breathe, Ava. You'll find another job, and maybe that one just wasn't for you anyway." I can't mention Brian's name right now.

Her eyes continue to fill up.

"My friend Russell was saying he was looking for someone to help him out with all his rental properties."

Ava tilts her head to the side. "You're so sweet. But I know you're making that up."

I am, but I could make it real. "No, I swear." I cross my heart, and I get a smile.

"What would I have to do, clean and stuff?"

"No. No, maybe show people the properties, get contracts signed, and stuff like that."

"I'm not qualified." Ava tucks her long, tanned legs under her.

"You said it yourself when I met you. You're a people person. So this would be interacting with lots of people."

She chews her lips, but I can see her bending. "Well, if the job is going. Yeah." Her smile widens, and I kiss her gently on the lips.

"I ordered pizza."

"You are going to make me fat."

My mind goes to a child growing in her stomach, and I wipe it away quickly. The idea is way too appealing to me.

"You're perfect," I tell her as the doorbell rings. I get our food, and we sit down on the couch to eat, chatting but not talking about what happened, and it's nice. Ava's funny, and she makes me laugh. She makes talking easy.

CHAPTER TWENTY

CONNOR

L AST NIGHT, I BARELY slept. My adrenaline was running too high. I'm not used to sitting and waiting, but on this, I have to. After breakfast, I drop Ava off at the hospital. Once she's finished, she promises me she will go straight home. She won't have any problems, because now I let myself focus on Brian and what he did to her as I drive to Kells.

"Neill, I was wondering if I could drop around soon for a chat. You still at your ma's?"

"Yeah, sure, Connor. I'll be here."

"See you soon." I hang up as I pull in beside Smyth's pub. It's locked. I snagged Ava's phone when she showered this morning and got Patrick's number out of it.

"Hello?"

"Patrick. It's Connor O'Reagan. I'm looking for Brian."

Movement at an upstairs window has me glancing up. Patrick lets the curtain fall back into place.

"I haven't seen him. But if I do, I'll let you know."

"I want to hurt him for putting his hands on Ava." I know Patrick likes Ava, so he might be more willing to cooperate.

"You have my word, Connor. That animal deserves to be put down."

Cars zoom past, and I have to wait a moment before I can cross the road. "Thanks Patrick." I climb into the car before pulling out and making my way to Neill's house. His mother answers the door. She's a large woman, and only at four foot.

She shuffles away from the door. "Connor, how are you?"

I have to move one foot in front of the other as she makes a slow path to the kitchen. "I'm good, Mrs O'Reilly. You look great," I say once we reach the kitchen. I plant a kiss on her cheek, and she swipes me away.

"You'll have a cup of tea."

"I wouldn't leave without one." I tell her, and she clicks on the kettle. Her body jiggles as she continues to laugh.

"I'll have one too, Ma." Her smile remains for her only son, Neill.

"Did you sleep well?" she asks him, forcing a kiss on his lips, which he wipes off.

"Jesus, Ma," he whines as he jumps up on the chair across from me.

"Doesn't like me kissing him in front of his friends," she tells me.

"I'm more like family."

Mrs. O'Reilly gives me a cup and a kiss that I accept.

"Jesus, Ma, would you stop." Neill takes his cup, and when his mam kisses him, he wipes his cheek.

"I'll leave you boys to it."

"Thanks, Mrs. O'Reilly," I say, raising my cup in salute as she closes the kitchen door.

"So what gives?"

"I got Mark yesterday," I tell him and watch him closely.

"Ah, nice one, Connor. You're a real pal."

"Yeah. I am, aren't I?"

He puts his finger in his ear and shakes it rapidly. "Yeah, that's what I just said." He shrugs and laughs before taking a drink of his tea.

"Funny story is that Mark said Brian paid him to attack you."

Neill's complexion pales, and when he starts stuttering, I give him a warning look. I don't want to hurt him.

"Yeah, he did. I didn't want to say anything, because it's messy."

I don't speak. Sometimes when you remain silent, the other person will keep talking just to fill the silence.

"Brian hates me because I ratted him out to Shane."

"You're a snitch for Shane?"

Neill holds up his hands. "No, no. I'd do it for any of you. You know that."

"Cut the bullshit, Neill. What did you tell Shane about Brian?"

"Brian was talking to a new supplier. I told Shane, and Shane beat the shit out of Brian. So in retaliation, he got me beat up."

"You pulled me into this mess. Why not ring Shane to come and save you after you were attacked?"

Neill tilts his head to the side. "You know he wouldn't have cared." Neill was right, but that didn't soften the betrayal of him lying to me.

"Do you know where Brian is now?"

"No, I swear." Neill holds up his hands again, like that meant shit.

"I don't even know if I believe you anymore."

"Connor, come on, man."

I stand, done with this conversation.

"You're going to hurt me?" Neill has his head in his hands.

"No, Neill. I don't hurt my friends," I tell him before leaving his house. I had thought of Neill as a friend, but this is a reminder that I can't trust anyone.

I take the piece of paper out of the glove compartment. My stomach twists. I'm ringing with no news, and I hate that. My only hope is that my dad has news for me.

"Hi, son. How is everything up there?"

His voice washes over me, and it makes me feel even more conflicted. I want to go back up north, but I'm not ready to leave Ava.

"A mess, to be honest."

"Not our mess?" He questions.

"No, Da, it's Darragh." I cut off, knowing we only have a certain amount of time and that he doesn't care about Darragh.

"No sign of Bernard and no word. What about you?" My stomach twists as I wait.

"Nothing. Call me when you have news." He hangs up, and his way sometimes reminds me too much of Michael's.

I ring Russell and try not to focus on my father's similarities to Michael.

"Man, I'll fix up with you soon for the apartment," I tell him, and he sounds like he's near traffic.

"No problem, Connor. All's good."

"I'm looking for another favor. I need a job. Like an auctioneer job."

Russell laughs. "You an auctioneer? You'd scare off all my punters."

I tut. "Not me, you dick. Ava. The girl in your apartment."

"You're telling me she doesn't have a job?"

I glare at Neill's house as I speak. "She just lost it. So I promised her I would get her one. Can you make that happen?"

"Not with me, Connor, but Gunnes is looking for one. Does she have qualifications?"

"No, but she's a real charmer."

Russell laughs. "She must be since you're pulling so many favors for her. Look, leave it with me, and I'll see what I can do."

"Okay. Don't leave it too long."

I take one final look at Neill's house before leaving the estate and making my way home. I better show my face after disappearing last night.

CHAPTER TWENTY ONE

AVA

T HE TAXI DROPS ME off. I'm trying to juggle my bag and pay the taxi man when my phone vibrates. "Thanks again," I say before I make my way into the apartment. Once my bag is on the counter, I check my phone. My heart deflates. It's Patrick. I was hoping to hear from Connor.

I want to send you your payment. Can you forward me your address? Hope you're keeping well.

It feels silly to make him post it out, but I'm not sure I'll be returning there anytime soon. I wish I could tell him I'd get it another time, but with everything going on, I need the money.

5 Headfort Demesne. Thanks, Patrick.

I'm trying to keep a positive mind set as I look around the apartment. It's more than I could ever have dreamed of. I just hope I get a job and am able to keep it.

My phone vibrates again.

Sure thing.

The wording is odd for Patrick, but he never texts, so maybe he's trying out some new phrases. The rubbish is only a bag, but I gather it up and take the keys out to the rubbish area. The white shutter gates are snow white. They look recently painted, and when I open them up, two large bins sit nearly side by side, one green and the other blue. I dump the rubbish into the recycling bin before heading back to the apartment.

As I clean, I keep checking my phone, hoping Connor will text. It's at such an odd moment—when I'm cleaning the bathroom—that I realize I love him. I'm in love with him. That crept up on me. Green eyes stare back at me, and I almost don't recognize the girl I see. She's smiling, yet hiding the mark on her face. My gaze drops to the floor, and I swallow the bile that rises in my throat. I'm too much work. He'll leave.

Your mother left you.

The ugly voice I shut down long ago is speaking up again, and I'm shaking my head in denial.

I repeat my nan's words. "It's her loss, not mine." My eyes water and I close them, not wanting to spill anymore tears. "It's her loss, not mine." I repeat it like a mantra until someone knocks on the door. I quickly pull myself together.

Connor.

I open the door and immediately try to slam it. Brian's hand grips the doorframe, and he forces it open. I throw my full weight behind it and slam the door on his hand. He lets go, but his roars have me rushing the door again. My head hits the wall as the door is busted open. The hallway darkens as Brian slams the door behind him. My head rings, and even as he approaches me, I can't seem to focus or move.

He pushes me into the living room, and I stumble onto the floor. I'm trying to stop the ringing in my head as Brian gets a towel for his bleeding hand. *My phone.*

I'm scrabbling, trying to get to my feet. I sway, but my hearing seems to have cleared.

"Sit down, Ava."

"Have you lost your mind?" I can't reason with this madness. He ignores me and points to the couch. I sit down, not wanting to gain any more injuries.

"It was you—" I shake my head at my own stupidity. "You pretended to be Patrick." He doesn't confirm or deny. Brian cradles his arm to his chest.

"Is your head okay?" He's a psycho.

My phone's on the counter, and I know if I can distract him for a minute, I could grab it and run.

"Yeah, it's fine," I answer, looking around the room for anything I could use as a weapon.

"Aren't you going to ask me if my hand's okay?"

I hope you bleed to death. "What do you want?"

He laughs, and I pull in a large gulp of air. "What I've always wanted, Ava. You."

"You had me, and you hurt me." Shivers race all over me as I say it. My bottom lip trembles, and I bite down to try to stop the emotion.

"Give me another chance." He's on his knees, making his way over to me. My vision blurs as I shake my head.

"Brian, please," I beg as he reaches me. Don't touch me.

"I was foolish to throw away what we had." He's looking at me like there's hope. I blink, and my vision clears fully as tears stream down my face.

"Okay," I say.

"Really?" He leans out like he doesn't quite believe me. I can only nod, and my throat closes up.

"You wouldn't lie to me, would you?"

"Of course not." I wipe my face with the sleeve of my top, trying to stem the flow of tears. "You're right. We were good together."

He's nodding, and my heart slams repeatedly against my chest. "Look at the mess you made of my hand."

Salty tears find their way into my mouth. "I'm so sorry. I just panicked."

"Yeah, you weren't expecting me. Were you expecting someone else?"

"No. I was just cleaning."

He stands now and looks around. "It's a nice place, Ava. A bit above your pay grade, but we'll make it work." My eyes snap to my phone, but I look away when he glances back at me.

"You want your phone?" he asks, and a sob falls from my mouth.

"No," I tell him. The ringing of my phone makes me jump. Brian picks it up, and I stand.

"Connor," Brian says as he scratches his head. He doesn't hang up or answer it. Instead, he places the phone on the counter.

Oh God. "Brian, we're just friends."

"Shut the fuck up, you slut!" he screams. I sit back down, rigid. "You have no intentions of getting back with me, do you?"

I want to lie down and close my eyes and pretend this isn't happening. If I say I do, he'll know I'm lying. If I say I don't, he'll lose it. I focus on the hardwood floor under my feet.

"Brian, please," I plead instead, but he's in front of me again, his bloody hand gripping my face.

"You're the only one I ever told about my childhood. You're the only person I've ever opened up to. I'm so in love with you, Ava. You have to see that." He told me about how his parents were addicts and he raised himself. Often hungry and afraid, he had to fend on his own. His story broke my heart, and all I ever wanted to do was help him. Heal him.

In a way, I did. He grew stronger, more confident. And then I became his punching bag. That, I could never forgive. I can't form the words, and I can't stop the flow of tears.

His fingers grip my hair painfully. "Answer me." Spit flecks across my face as he screams.

"If you loved me, you would have never hurt me. You're hurting me now."

His grip loosens, but he doesn't let me go. "Do you love me?"

I close my eyes until his hold tightens on my hair. My heart is jumping around my chest, making its way into my throat. I need this to end. "No, Brian, I don't love you anymore."

He releases me, and a sob tears from my throat. His blue eyes shine with tears, and I'm stiff, getting ready for the blow that he will no doubt land on me. But he doesn't. Something in him softens, and he moves into my personal space. "Kiss me."

"What?" I'm not sure I heard him right, but he leans in and tries to brush his lips against mine. My hands move on reflex and slam against his chest, stopping his progression.

"No, Brian. Just stop." Hitting me is one thing; forcing himself on me is unthinkable. He pushes against me, his lips roughly touching mine. I lash out and scratch his face, ready to bolt. I don't get to move. His large hands encircle mine as he pins me to the ground.

"What the fuck are you doing?" I'm shouting my panic, pleading with the rational part of him. "Don't do this." I can barely breathe as he leans down and kisses me again. My brain is screaming that this can't be real. Somewhere in the background, my phone rings, a reminder that this is very much real, and if I don't get up, the unthinkable is going to happen.

He's screaming, trying to pull away from me, but I've locked my jaw after sinking my teeth into his lip. My hands are free, and it's a moment of relief until his fist connects with the side of my head.

Darkness swamps me, and the taste of iron fills my mouth. I try to spit out the liquid, but the weight is still on top of me. I buck blindly, but everything gets heavier, and I slow down. The burn on the back of my neck jerks me. Cold air brushes my skin.

"No, don't." It's weak. I need to open my eyes. I need to stop this. The weight is lifted, and my stomach hollows out as rough hands tug at my trousers. My vision clears, and I'm sideways. Brian is opening his jeans.

Move, Ava.

"You're a stupid bitch and a slut." His words wake me up a bit more. I move, and he grips my bare thighs painfully. I kick out my legs and connect with his shoulder. His face is a bloody mess, but I still see the snarl as his hands dig into my legs, making their way back up to me.

"Get away from me." My throat burns as I scream and thrash under him. He grabs one of my swinging hands, but not before I drag my nails down his face.

"Fuck's sake, Ava."

"Help. Help." I can't get his weight off me. Wriggling under him is only aggravating him more, but I can't give up. This can't be it.

His face is close to mine, but he's not stupid enough to try to kiss me again. I spit at him, and pain explodes down the side of my face as his temper flares again.

I'm trying to stay awake. Brian is still on top of me, his head tilted to the side, and I don't know what he's listening to until I hear it, and my throat tightens, and my eyes blur. Someone is knocking on the door.

"Help! Please!" A sweaty hand clamps down on my face, and I bite hard, refusing to let go. Brian's roars pound in my head.

I spit when Brian tears his hand back. The knocking is now gone, and it sounds like someone is throwing themselves against the door. Brian gets off me, his eyes roaming the room. The wooden floor scratches my hands as I move backward. My back hits the couch, and I cling to it. My top is torn. On the floor, my trousers are near the door. The rattle of the door has me glancing at Brian.

He takes out a knife, and I shake my head. The world explodes as the front door shatters in on top of us. Brian moves quickly toward me, and I'm trying to scurry across the couch. My body is limp like I've been drugged, and I scream at it to move. My head whips around at the sound of running feet. I pause as a sob tears itself free from my throat.

Connor.

His pause is so brief, but my eyes connect with his, and something shifts between us, but I can't stop the crying. The sound that's leaving me doesn't sound like me. When Connor releases me from his stare, he's moving mechanically toward Brian.

Someone else enters the room, but my focus is on Connor. Brian swipes. Connor jumps back and disarms him in a second. The knife skitters across the floor before Connor punches Brian in the face. The impact seems to shake the floor under me as Brian hits the ground hard.

"Wait, let me explain. She came on to me," Brian says. Connor stands over him as he tries to crawl away. I don't turn away as a heavy boot slams into Brian's face. The crunch of his nose is satisfying. Connor's over Brian now, his fist slamming into Brian's face repeatedly. I can't take my eyes away from Connor. He's transformed. He's savage in his attack, and I don't want him to stop. I don't want him to ever stop.

"Connor." The person with Connor is trying to pull him off, gripping his arm. It slows Connor down but doesn't stop him. "You need to stop."

The other guy doesn't sound overly alarmed, but his words break through the walls Connor built around himself. He stops, his hands a bloody mess. Brian is unrecognisable under him. Brown eyes that are almost black hold mine, and Connor's moving again. Releasing Brian, he moves over to me.

"Get me a blanket," he demands. The other guy leaves the room as Connor takes me in his arms, cradling me against his chest like a child, and I release a flood of tears.

"It's okay." His whispered words are accompanied by a blanket being wrapped around me. He's standing still, holding me in his arms, and then he sits.

"What about him?"

"Just give me a minute." Connor's words rumble through his chest. My hands tighten on his top as I push my face deeper into his chest.

"It's okay," he tells me again. I stay in my safe cocoon until the other man speaks again.

"Didn't realize he was such a fucking maniac." Smoke makes its way into my safe place. Peeking out, I see the other boy is smoking. His eyes clash with mine.

"Hi." He gives me a nod. I don't answer him but look up into familiar brown eyes.

"He's my brother. He's here to help."

I nod and swallow another flood of emotions. "How did you know?" My throat is hoarse.

"Will you get me some water?" Connor asks his brother before looking down at me. "Patrick rang me when I was at home. He told me that Brian attacked him and made him get your address."

His brother arrives back with the water and hands it to Connor, who holds it to my lips. I take a deep gulp. My eyes want to move to the left, where Brian still lies, his body still, but I focus on bloody hands and brown eyes. His gentle touch is a contradiction to the savagery he just displayed.

"You okay for a minute?" he asks me.

I'm nodding, but my body is screaming, Don't go. Don't leave me. I start to tremble, and he wraps the blanket tighter around my shoulders.

"Ring Russell," he says to his brother. "Tell him we need a new front door. I'll move him." He plants a kiss on my head.

Brian is dragged by his arms across the wooden floor. His head rocks every time it hits something. But Connor doesn't slow his pace as he drags him out of the room. I don't care if he's dead. I tighten the blanket as Connor's brother gives a half smile as he rings Russell. A cigarette dangles from his mouth. I can't manage to smile back, so I focus on the door to the hallway as I wait for Connor to come back. Two hundred forty-five seconds later, he returns empty-handed.

"He'll be here within the hour," the brother tells Connor, who nods.

"He's in the trunk. I need you to make sure he doesn't get out."

"No problem." Before his brother passes him, Connor clamps a hand on his shoulder. "Thanks, Darragh."

Darragh nods at Connor. "I got you," he tells Connor, who releases him and returns to me.

Connor picks me up softly and carries me into the bedroom. After sitting me on the bed, he moves around silently, pulling the curtains and closing the bedroom door. The shower is turned on, and when Connor reappears, he still doesn't focus on me. He's rummaging through my drawers, taking out clean clothes and placing them on the bed beside me before he turns his attention to me. Removing the blanket, I shiver.

"I can walk," I tell him when he tries to pick me up. My legs wobble like jelly, but I make it to the bathroom. It feels like a dream as I remove my underwear and bra and step into the spray of water. The heat rattles my body, and I hold on to the wall. I want to scream into the white tiles, scream all the rage that's built up inside me. Soft hands touch my back, and I glance at Connor over my shoulder. He's naked behind me, the water hitting his chest.

"Let me help you?" he asks, and I nod as he soaps up a cloth and washes every inch of my skin. The care, the gentleness, nearly undoes me again after my body has felt such abuse. His hands still on each mark, and I realize there's a lot. I haven't seen my face, but it aches, and each touch burns away the roots of darkness that Brian planted. Each touch releases the knots in my chest. Each touch is making me remember that Brian didn't succeed, because Connor stopped him.

"Thank you."

He freezes, and I look up at Connor, blinking as the spray keeps interfering with my view. But the pain in his eyes catches my breath.

CHAPTER TWENTY TWO

CONNOR

SHE'S ASLEEP IN BED, and I can't seem to find the strength to leave her. But the idea of getting to hurt Brian all over again has me slipping from her room. Russell had a new door put on and is gone now. Outside, Darragh sits on the boot of the car smoking a cigarette. Opening the front door, he turns to me and w   a   l   k   s over.

"I need you to stay with her."

"I'm not that good with women," Darragh says as he throws the fag on the ground.

"She's asleep, and I can't leave her alone."

Darragh nods. "Yeah, go on. What do I say if she wakes up?"

"Tell her I've taken Brian to Navan Gardaí station. But if she wants to talk to me, just ring me."

"You're not really taking him to Navan, are you?"

I don't answer his question but pat him on the back.

"Thanks, Darragh. I owe you one," I tell him, handing him the set of keys.

He takes it with a grin. "Just be careful."

***

I drive to Kells—an old bakery that's closed down, and is owned by Michael. It was in the works to be turned into flats, but right now, it's abandoned. The locks are easy to break as I push up the shutter and back the car into the space. Pulling the shutter back down, we're plunged into the darkness. Once I'm back in the car, I turn on the car lights.

The area is open, with large cement pillars. I veer the car around. Large plastic sheeting hangs from one wall, where they started reconstruction but had to stop. Some people in the town objected to the bakery being turned into flats. It's still tied up in legal issues, but no doubt Michael will bribe whoever he needs to. My gloves sit along with my gun in the glove compartment. I remove both and put them on.

The sheet of plastic pulls away easily, and I drag it to the middle of the room, keeping it within the range of my car lights. Thumping sounds come from the boot.

"Good. Just in time," I tell Brian as I open the boot. He glares up at me, trying to cover his face. I don't give him a moment but drag him from the boot.

He hits the ground heavily, and I grab one leg and drag him toward the plastic. His cries and pleas don't make me pause. Once he's deposited on the plastic, I return to the car and get my gun before turning on the music. Country music blares from the speakers. The noise has Brian looking around him. One eye is sealed. The other darts around the space before he stares at the plastic under his hands.

"No, man." He's shaking his head. Blood drips from his face.

I kneel down in front of him, and he looks at me.

"Please." His teeth are red with blood.

"Did Ava say please?" I ask, and he drops my gaze. "You know what this is?" I hold up the gun in my hand. His one eye flickers around the space again.

"A gun."

"Well done, Brian. It's not just a gun. It's a silencer. So no one will hear when I empty it into you."

Horror has his eyes widening, and I soak up his fear. "It's not fair, me with the gun and you with nothing." I tell him while tucking the gun into the back of my jeans.

"Since you like beating on women, I'm going to give you a chance. You fight me, and I'll let you go."

"I can't win." Tears make a pathway down his face.

"You don't want to try?" I ask, taking the gun back out and pointing it at his forehead. His hands rise into the air.

"Jesus. Please, I'll do anything you want. This isn't just about Ava, is it? It's about Harry?"

I don't respond but let him talk.

"I'll tell him to back off."

I'm standing now, my finger trigger ready. "Don't mention her name again," I tell him, and he looks up but ducks his head down again while keeping his hands in the air.

"I won't. I'm sorry."

"Why did you get men to beat up Neill?"

"He told Shane I was trying to do a deal with a new guy, and Shane beat me up. So I got Neill beaten up."

"Would you do that to me, Brian? Would you hire men to hurt me if I let you live?" I'm on my hunkers again, and he's shaking his head.

"I swear I'd disappear. You'd never see me again."

"You mentioned Harry? Tell me about the deal you have with him."

He's more alert now, maybe thinking he needs to be careful. A wave of my gun has him making his mind up quickly.

"I told Harry about the body we buried in the bog."

Ah, so we have our rat.

"You helped Shane bury a body?"

He's nodding. One mangled hand reaches up and wipes blood from his chin.

"The dealer who tried to move in on his turf—they knew each other. And Brendan, I think his name was, made a reference about Shane's mother. He lost it and killed the guy."

I lean out as Brian's eye starts to close. His words send dread dripping down my back.

"Describe Brendan to me."

He shakes his head and whimpers. A slap to his face has him speaking again. "Tall, brown hair, Northern Ireland accent. I think he was attached to the IRA. Yeah. He mentioned the IRA."

I'm standing and walking away from Brian before returning.

"Bernard," I say more to myself.

"Yeah, yeah. Not Brendan—Bernard. He was his cousin or something. Look, I'll tell Harry to drop it."

I'm kneeling again as my heart tries to break free from my rib cage. "You saw Shane kill Bernard?"

He's nodding. "Look, I can unsee it. You know what I mean."

I'm standing again. Shane killed my brother.

"How did he kill him?"

Brian tries to stand, and I send him sailing back to the ground. Red splatters across the plastic as he coughs up blood.

"Answer me." He's on his side now, his breaths fogging up the plastic under him.

"Bernard made a statement about his father being with his mother. He lost it and hit him." Brian rolls onto his back, his breathing becoming deeper.

"Bernard hit his head. I think that's what killed him. It was an accident."

I'm picturing Bernard dying at the hands of Shane.

"Where did this happen?"

Brian starts to whimper again and pleads with me to take him to a hospital.

"I will. You have my word. I'll take you to the hospital. Just answer me."

"You're lying," Brian cries.

"Nah, you have my word."

"Smyth's," he tells me with a snivel.

I'm struggling to wrap my mind around this. Shane killed my brother.

"Was anything else said between them?" I ask, and Brian looks panicked as he scurries to think. I don't think Shane knows I'm Bernard's brother. But Bernard mentioning Mam and Tom together is odd.

"No, that's it."

I nod, and Brian starts crying.

"Can I go now?"

"You really think I will let you go after what you did to Ava?"

"I told you everything."

"You did. But you're still going to die."

I don't hesitate as I put three bullets in Brian's body. One in each kneecap before firing the last one between his eyes. Blood pools fast, and I move, grabbing the plastic and tightening it around his body. I grab a silver roll of duct tape from the car and tie both ends until the roll is gone. I drag Brian to the car and get him into the boot before I let the betrayal sink in.

I need to tell Da, but I also know what he would want me to do. The area looks clear as I make one final sweep of the room before getting into the car and lowering the music. I remove the gloves and gun and put them into the glove compartment. Then I make a phone call.

"How is she?" I ask the moment Darragh answers.

"She's asleep."

I'm nodding as I start to reverse up to the shutters. "Okay. I might be a few more hours. You good there?"

"Yeah, you do what you need to do."

I end the call and jump out of the car and push up the shutter. The light has me blinking after the stark darkness of the bakery. Traffic moves by in the same pattern as it always does. People walk up and down the street, and it all feels normal. Pulling out the car, I close the shutter.

Can you put a lock on the bakery shutter on John's street? My dad owns it, and I see someone broke it. I'll sort you out soon for everything, man. Thanks.

I'm driving toward home, trying to think of my next move. I need to get rid of the body in my car. I can burn out the car later. Getting Brian out of the boot is vital. The Loch Leigh Mountains spring to mind, but I think of a better place. When I arrive home, I curse myself. My hands are caked in blood, so I wash my hands in the sink, the last of the red liquid disappearing down the drain.

"Hey, have you seen Darragh?" I dry my hands while turning to Finn.

"He's on a job. Don't worry, he's fine." Finn stares at me, and now I wonder if I have blood on my face.

"You okay?"

"Yeah, just out last night." I throw the paper towel into the bin.

"With Darragh? That will give you one hell of a hangover." Finn's grinning, and I just want him to leave.

"Mother of all hangovers," I tell him. Finn walks with me as I go to my room. "Shower and some sleep." I grin, and he smirks at me.

"And you have Darragh working today?" He laughs.

I close the door and lean against it for a moment before opening it. Checking the hall confirms that Finn is gone, and I make my way back to the garage. The hum of the engine sounds like it's roaring, and I pull out of the garage and make my way to the back of the house. I grab supplies from the shed and then throw them into the back seat before I drive around the sheds and out of sight.

I sit and wait an agonizing twenty minutes. I just need to make sure no one saw me. When the twenty minutes are up, I leave the sheds and drive across the fields toward the forest. I keep to the outline of the forest until the field is cut off by a ditch. Veering into it, I drive as far as the forest will allow. I'm not very deep, but I'm hidden. This would be handy with another person, but I'm on my own.

I drag Brian across the forest floor until my arms ache and burn. When I look around me, I can't see anything but trees. Returning to the car, I get out the shovels and the black paint and brush. I pull my body up high into a large oak tree and paint a thick layer of black paint onto the trunk. It will be my only marking of where he is buried.

The burn in my arms is severe as I continue to dig. I'm only halfway down when I have to stop. A tremble has entered my hands. My limbs aren't cooperating anymore. My stomach lifts, and I close my eyes, trying to make it settle. I've never killed anyone before, and it scares me how easy it was. Brian deserved to die. The thought of him hurting Ava has me continuing to dig until the hole is deep enough. Clay crumbles under my fingers as I pull myself out of the grave. My boot connects with Brian's body as I kick and push him toward the grave. The heavy thud is satisfactory, and the plastic soon disappears under the grave of clay.

I don't stop at the house but make my way back to Ava.

CHAPTER TWENTY THREE

AVA

MY HEART POUNDS, AND a pool of sweat sits on my chest. My mind is jumping around, not settling on anything. Water spraying on my body, gentle hands, Brian's roars, Connor's rage. I tighten my eyes to stop it all and sit up. My stomach twists painfully. My abused face screams at me, and my head pounds. I don't move as tears stream down my face. He tried to rape me. The thought of his rough fingers has me swallowing bile. I can't stay here. I'm out of the bed and pausing at the door. The smell of smoke has my stomach twisting again.

Connor's brother. It's only Connor's brother.

The door opens slowly, and I step out into the living space. Blue eyes focus on me. He doesn't speak and neither do I. I tighten my arms around my waist.

"Where is Connor?" My throat burns and I clear it. Darragh is up now, moving toward the kitchen. I don't move but watch him. I hate how I flinch when he walks toward me with a glass of water. It takes me a moment to take it from him.

"He'll be back soon." He smiles, but I nod and give him a wide berth as I move to the couch and sit down. He stays standing, giving me some space, and that makes me relax a bit more.

"Thank you." I take a deep drink of water, and it feels nice on my aching throat.

"So, you and Connor are dating?"

I shrug. I'm not sure how to answer that question. I don't know what me and Connor are. "I don't know," I finally answer, and Darragh leans against the wall.

"How did you meet?" Darragh checks his phone, and I feel his questions are to keep me occupied.

"Where I work and then later in the supermarket. He asked me out for coffee."

"Can't picture Connor in a supermarket." Darragh grins, and I find myself smiling.

"Yeah. He was buying Swiss Rolls," I tell Darragh, and he laughs. His brother being here reminds me of how little I know about Connor's life. "Do you live with Connor?"

"Yeah, in Whitewood House. None of us have fled the nest yet."

I've heard of Whitewood House. Surprise flitters through me at the knowledge that Connor lives there.

Darragh's phone rings, and I don't know which of us is more relieved. Our conversation is strained. Right now, all I want is Connor. Darragh smiles at me.

"He's here now." He leaves and opens the front door. The overwhelming urge to cry bubbles up in my throat when Connor walks into the room. His eyes land on me.

"You're awake?" He's beside me, pulling me into his arms, and I let him.

"Yeah. I feel a bit better," I say. Soft lips brush my forehead. Darragh moves across from us and sits down.

"You get all sorted?" he asks Connor, and Connor's arms stiffen around me.

"Yeah."

I'm looking up into brown eyes. "What did you do with Brian?" I really want to ask if he's still alive. He didn't look so good when he was dragged from here. Now that I look around the living area, I don't see a trace of what happened. I wonder if it was Darragh or Connor who cleaned it up.

"I took him to Navan Gardaí station."

My throat closes, and I nod. "They need me to make a statement." This is the part I hate.

"Not right now. He's being held on a list of charges. I think it will be a long time before Brian gets out."

"Did they tell you when they need me to go in? I'd prefer to do it when I visit Nan soon. Get it done and over with."

"They didn't say, but please don't worry about it."

I am going to worry about it, but for right now, I nod.

"I'm going to take the car and head home," Darragh tells Connor. "Is that okay?"

"Yeah, that's fine. Maybe you could air her out when you get home." Something passes between the brothers, and Darragh stands.

"I can do that." Darragh takes the keys from Connor. "Ava, you take care of yourself."

I smile at him for the first time. "Thank you for everything, Darragh. I don't know what I would have done if you and Connor hadn't arrived." My voice closes on the last words, and Darragh shifts uncomfortably.

"Don't mention it," he says, giving me a salute as he leaves the room. Once the front door is closed, I sink further into Connor.

"I don't want you to be scared, Ava. He's gone now, okay?"

I turn in Connor's arms so I'm looking at him. His fingers move across my cheek.

"You know what was even scarier?" My lip trembles, and I bite it. "Losing you. I'm waiting for the other shoe to drop—" My words are cut off as Connor presses his lips against mine. His kiss weaves its way through my veins, rushing all the way to my toes.

"I'm not going anywhere." His words against my lips have me opening my eyes.

My heart is galloping, and my pulse flickers in my neck. "I'm falling in love with you, Connor." I'm in love with you.

Connor's smile is instant, and it's a balm on a wound as he reaches me again and kisses me. I'm on his lap now, straddling him, and he's all I want. He's all I need.

I'm pushing my body against his, and he looks at me, his eyes a deep brown. His breath brushes my face. "Are you sure? We don't have to?"

I answer his question with a kiss. My fingers move under his shirt. Muscles coil under my touch. I let myself forget everything and lose myself in Connor.

***

We spend three days holed up in the apartment, blocking out the world, and it's perfect. Each morning, I wait for him to tell me he has to leave, but he doesn't. Every moment with Connor heals me.

"How about we get out today?" Connor is eating toast at the breakfast bar. He's a sight for sore eyes with no top on. I could handle a few more days locked in here with him, but getting out would be nice too.

"Yeah, I suppose we can't stay in here forever." I pout, and my stomach twists as Connor smiles at me.

"Did you ring your nan?" He puts the toast in my mouth, and I take a bite.

"Yep, told her I was bogged down with a new job. She's doing good."

Connor takes another bite of toast. "Speaking of jobs, my friend Russell was wondering when you can start. Gunnes has a position if you want it." I jump into his arms because he's the best.

"Thank you so much." I kiss him before stealing his toast.

"Maybe you could thank me tonight."

I'm grinning. "We'll see," I tell Connor, but I couldn't keep away from him even if I wanted to.

***

It's weird to be walking the streets of Kells. When people look at me, I think the marks on my face are visible and immediately duck my head.

A warm hand squeezes mine. "You're beautiful, Ava," Connor tells me as he stops us on the street. He's moved me into his arms now and kisses me. When we break apart, I blush knowing we're being watched. We walk around the town hand in hand. Passing Smyth's makes me stiffen, but once we're around the corner, I relax. We are coming up to the café where we had our first date.

"Connor," I say, but I don't get his attention. Connor's hand has tightened on mine painfully, and when I yank my hand, he releases me.

"Sorry." He's distracted looking at someone as they jog across the road.

When he gets to us, the guy says, "I was ringing your phone the last few days."

The silence from Connor has me glancing at him, and his eyes flicker to me, searching my face before he answers. "I saw that. I was tied up."

The other guy smiles at me. Brown eyes similar to Connor's look at me. "Aren't you going to introduce me to your beautiful friend?" The compliment is said with an outstretched hand, and I take it.

"I'm Ava," I tell him, since Connor seems to have lost the ability to speak.

"Shane. Connor's brother."

Ah, that explains the eyes. Connor said he didn't get on with Shane. Maybe that's why he's acting so weird.

"What do you want?" Connor's rude words have me releasing Shane's hand.

"Can't one brother worry about the other?" Shane widens his eyes at me, a kind smile on his face, and I feel embarrassed at how rude Connor is being.

"We were just about to grab a coffee," I say and can feel Connor's heavy stare on my shoulders.

"I would love to join you," Shane says.

"Great." I nudge Connor, and once again, my movements seem to relax him a bit more.

***

Awkward isn't enough to describe how it feels as we sit in the booth. Connor sits beside me, Shane across from us.

"So are you dating?" he asks, and I smile.

"I'm not sure." I give him the same answer I gave Darragh.

"You should really put the girl out of her misery," Shane tells Connor as the waitress arrives. We order, and Shane returns to prodding Connor. "You're all uptight, Connor. Relax."

Connor stiffens even more at Shane's words, and we sit in silence as our coffees arrive.

"So are you from the area?" Shane asks me.

"Yeah, born and raised here."

"Shane, you should leave," Connor says.

Jesus, Connor is being so rude, but it isn't my place to intervene. Shane shrugs out of his coat and pushes up the sleeves of his jumper. Something in me stills. The air feels tight, and my eyes trace the black bands on his arms. My memory snaps back to the night in the pub. My hand jerks, knocking my coffee all over the table. We all move, and I'm apologizing as my mind races.

"Are you okay?" Connor is cleaning up the spill with napkins, but Shane is watching me. I can't look up at Connor.

"Yeah," I answer. The waitress arrives and starts to mop up the coffee. My chest grows tighter. "I'm just going to the bathroom." I don't wait for their dismissal.

He was with the missing boy—Shane. Shane is Connor's brother. Connor arrived into my pub—

I'm in the bathroom, the contents of my stomach coming up. Sitting on the ground, I kick the wall and lean my head against the far wall. Connor had asked me questions about Harry and the missing boy. My stomach heaves again. When I went to the Gardaí Station, he talked me out of reporting it.

Oh my God. My hand trembles as I cover my mouth. I can't go back out there. I can't let them see what they've done to me.

I'm up on my feet and making my way out of the small café. Ducking down, I cross the open space and glance at Connor and Shane. Their conversation is low and intense. The fresh air burns my eyes, and I dip my head as I make my way down the street. What if Connor doesn't know? What if I'm jumping to conclusions? I'm slowing down. The rational part of me is telling me that of course he knew. The circumstances were stacked too high. But my heart wants to believe that we met and fell in love, and the fact that I crossed paths with his brother before is just a coincidence

"Ava. Ava." Connor reaches me and grips my shoulders. "What's wrong?" The way he questions me makes it sound like he already knows.

"Please don't lie to me," I tell him. Connor releases me and joins his hands together.

"Everything okay?" Shane arrives, sliding on his jacket.

"Can you fuck off for five minutes?" Connor snaps, and Shane loses his smile.

"Fine. But know this, Connor. You did a good job." His words are like a nail in my coffin.

Am I the job?

My stomach churns again, and I start walking briskly. Connor tries to stop me. "Don't touch me," I say. I shrug him off as I clutch my stomach.

"You have to listen to me," he pleads.

Something in me cracks, and I stop walking. I can't look up at Connor. The pathetic part of me wants him to explain this away.

"It's not how he's making it sound."

My lip trembles. *So Shane wasn't lying... I am a job.*

"Like your brother said, you did a great job." I've felt a lot of pain in life, but this is different.

"Ava, I met you, and straight away I wanted you."

I glance up at Connor as my nose burns and my eyes fill. "How could you hurt me like this?" He knew my past; he knew about Brian. My job, my home, everything. "I can't even go back to my apartment because it's all yours."

He's shaking his head. "No, that's yours."

"Stop! Nothing is mine. You've manipulated and controlled everything." I laugh through my tears. "I feel so stupid." I inhale deeply to try to settle the hysteria that's bubbling up. "I loved you," I tell Connor, but he's shaking his head.

"I can fix this."

No, he can't. I turn away from him before I crumble here on the sidewalk. I gather the small bit of dignity I have left and walk. I have no idea where to. I still have my old apartment for a few more days.

"Ava, please just let me try."

I stop walking at the credit union and turn to Connor. "You've made me feel this small." I hold up two fingers close together. I'm glad when my words make him flinch. "I want you to feel what I'm feeling." A sob tears from my throat, and Connor's eyes glaze.

"I do. I'm so sorry. Jesus. I was going to tell you, I swear. But it just never felt like the right time."

"Yeah, I can't imagine telling someone you only stepped into their life to find out information about them could slot neatly into some timeframe." I'm shouting. I don't care that people are watching. My skin feels tight.

"Get away from me." I wipe angrily at my tears.

"I love you, Ava." His words make me cry because only half an hour ago, that's all I would have wanted to hear. Those three little words would have made my world complete. Now they make me angry.

"I need you to leave me alone," I tell Connor, and he doesn't move.

"I need to make sure you're home safely. I promise I'll give you space then."

"*No*." Then it clicks with me, and I'm really looking at him. "What happens to me now? Is someone going to hurt me?" I cover my mouth, wondering what the hell I've gotten myself into.

"No one, and I mean no one, will ever put their hands on you again. You have my word." Connor's holding my arms, and I shrug him off, but his words ease the worry in me, because they ring true to me. "Just let me get you home safely."

I'm nodding because I don't know what to do. I fold my arms across my chest as Connor rings a taxi so we can get into town, as Darragh took his car. My cheeks heat. Did Darragh know? I wonder now if they all sat around a table and laughed at the stupid girl.

"He'll be here soon."

I don't acknowledge Connor or speak to him as we make our way back to Headfort Demesne—such a shattered dream. I hold it together as I get out of the taxi. I keep strong even as Connor walks me to the door.

"I'll give you space, but I'm not going anywhere, Ava."

"How noble of you, Connor," I tell him before closing the door in his face. I'm staring at it like it might explode inwards, but when the taxi pulls away, I let myself shatter as I pour my pain across the wooden floor.

CHAPTER TWENTY FOUR

CONNOR

"THANKS." I SLIP THE taxi man a fifty and walk up the pass to the house. I didn't want him to drop me at the door.

When I reach the house, Darragh's making his way out of the garage. He pulls up and rolls down his window. "What's up?"

"Not much." I shove my hands into my pockets. For the first time, I can't sort through all the shit that's going on inside me.

"Okay then." Darragh lights up a cigarette. "I aired your car for you."

"Thanks, I appreciate it. Now I need to find another one."

"You can use my Jeep if you want. Hate the fucking thing."

I grin at Darragh and tap the roof to let him go. "Thanks, man. I'll catch you later."

"Oh, be warned. Dad is on the warpath. That's why I'm evacuating."

I don't give a shit about Michael. I nod at Darragh and walk off as his car roars down the pass. Glancing across my shoulder, all I see is a cloud of dust.

"I can't do this anymore," I hear yelled.

If it were anyone else, I would go to my room. But it's Finn who's shouting. I find Michael, Liam, Shane, Una—who I'm surprised to see—and Finn in the library.

No one seems to notice my presence.

"Where is he now?" Michael's red face is tight with anger, and I step closer to Finn, getting Michael's attention.

"I'm fucking here, Michael," I tell him and sit close to Finn just in case.

"You're an impudent little pup."

I nod and smirk at him.

"The last time I checked, he was leaving," Finn says. "And honestly, I don't blame him."

"I have guards at my door, forensics digging up my land, yet I have four sons who can't seem to keep it together."

"Five sons, Michael." Una's voice sounds so quiet and sweet.

"What?" His voice has lowered, but it still holds a warning.

"You've five sons. You said four."

Michael doesn't answer her, but I feel all eyes on me.

"We acknowledge that something must be done." Liam speaks up, calmly and clearly. Michael rubs his face and sits down.

"This is not as bad as you think. The charges have been dropped against Darragh, and they found animal carcasses in the bog." Shane says, and I clench my fists.

"It is, Shane. Because Darragh is a loose cannon, and right now, we need a solution to this problem. I can't have guards on my doorstep. I've operated this business for over forty years, and I've never drawn their attention."

I can't stop staring at Shane, and he catches my eye a few times. *You killed my brother. You destroyed things with me and Ava.*

"If you're going to hit me, go ahead," Shane says. My message must have gotten across to him. He stands, wide arms outstretched like I'd attack him now.

I smirk at him. "Relax, Shane. I'm not going to hit you." I sit further back into the couch.

"You want to explain what's going on here?" Michael asks me, and I point at Shane.

"I'll let Shane tell you." It's like it dawns on him that my work for him was kept from his family. *Stupid fucker.*

"A misunderstanding," he says, and I laugh just to wind him up.

"You tell so many lies that you don't even know the truth." Una leans out and stares at me while tilting her head, and I meet her eye. I like Una.

"You should run," I tell her. "That's my advice to you."

"Leave her out of this." Shane's taking a step toward me, and I lean back again.

"No." I smirk again, and he clenches his fist.

"We have more important things to discuss," Michael says, and Shane steps away.

"That's a good boy," I tease him, but he doesn't bite.

Liam speaks up again. "Darragh will work for me. I take full responsibility for him."

"Darragh in a brothel?" Finn's looking doubtful.

"A Brothel?" Una says. "You work in a brothel?"

This is the first time I've ever seen Una react to something about the families work.

"Yes, I do." Liam's answer is said with a soft jerk of his head.

"Okay, I agree with that," Michael says, and Finn still looks doubtful but keeps his mouth shut. The responsibility is finally off his shoulders, and that makes me happy.

"But Finn, you still need to look out for him when he's here. It doesn't mean you can just walk away." Michael's eyes flicker to me before they return to Finn. "No one walks away from this family."

"I'm not walking away from this family. I'm getting married, and I want a life besides all this."

Michael shakes his head before looking at his two noble sons. "Family comes first." They nod like two soldiers.

Finn's face tightens as he taps his foot on the floor.

"Since I'm not family, I'm good to go." Rising, I wink at Una. I don't have to look at Shane to know it annoys the hell out of him.

Shit hurts at times. Like when you're walking down a hall and no one calls you back and says, "Stop, Connor, you are family." No, the only words that are shouted at me are from Shane.

"You're going to push me too far, Connor."

I haven't even started. Facing him makes me even angrier now, and he walks toward me with a smirk. Knowing his actions are roiling me just like I knew mine back in that room were roiling him.

"Are you really going to declare war over a girl?"

I'm smiling, telling myself to remain calm. "If you ran my dog down, that would be enough to declare a war with you. You're a vindictive, evil—" Una and Finn step out into the hall, and for them, I want to stop but for Ava and Bernard, I keep going.

"Murderer," I say the final word slowly. He doesn't like that at all. He's not shrinking away; he stands taller, like I've just handed him a knife.

"If you think I'm all that, then be careful."

"Come on, guys." Finn is trying to move in between us, but we're toe to toe.

"No, Finn, I'm not afraid," Shane says, and I push my forehead against his. I put all my anger and frustration into the action.

"Oh my God, guys, seriously?" Una says. I glance at her, and for the first time, I feel angry at her stupidity.

Stepping only a foot away from Shane, I stare at Una. "You know what they do?" Her face brightens. "Yet you still lie with him."

Rough hands grip my neck, and I'm slammed into the wall. "Stop speaking to her."

"Shane," Una warns, but I allow Shane to manhandle me.

"Una, I thought you had more respect for yourself," I say. Shane slams his fist into my stomach, knocking the wind from me. As I gasp for air, I start to laugh and cough. "You'll piss him off one day and end up in a ditch."

He charges, taking both of us to the ground. I allow each thump to my face. It fuels me. Liam and Finn pull Shane off me. I'm on my hands and knees, coughing as blood drips from my mouth and nose. When I look up, Una stares at me, a hand over her mouth as her eyes hold horror.

"I needed to show you what he is," I tell her, and Liam holds Shane back as I stand and wipe blood from my face. Michael's standing behind them all, staring hate at me.

"You must be so proud of your sons, Michael. You did a great job with them all."

"That's enough," Liam barks. His raised voice causes a lull to fall in the hall. More blood drops off my chin, and I wipe it away, but some hits the floor.

Una takes a step toward me with tears in her eyes. "Connor..." She's shaking her head, but I don't want her sympathy. I leave the front door open as I walk out of the house and make my way to the back. I need to cool down. My throat burns. No doubt Shane's hand marks are visible. I rub it, but it doesn't help.

"Connor." I want Finn to just stay inside. I don't need him coming after me. But he's there, and he's angry.

"Why did you let him hit you?"

I shrug, knowing exactly why I did it. I wanted everyone to see a monster, even just a glimpse. I wanted to put the seed of doubt into Una's head. It was a scratch to the surface compared to what I was going to do to him. No matter what, he would die. He had to. He took the life of my brother, the general's son.

"Connor, please talk to me." I stop walking and face the house. Too many windows to count look down on us. Any one of them could have an occupant.

"I wanted Una to see what he's really like."

"By letting him beat the crap out of you?"

I'm grinning now. "Darragh would have been impressed," I tell Finn, and he lets out an exasperated breath.

"Darragh would have been in the middle of it."

"Yeah, he would have. It would have been fuel on a fire."

"What happened between you two? It was never this bad before."

Stuffing my hands into my pockets, I try to stay as close to the truth as possible.

"He just messed up something good I had. With a girl. Her name's Ava."

"A girl?" Finn's smiling now, but I don't feel like smiling.

My stomach twists. What if she won't forgive me?

"Fight for her. Win her back."

"He really did a number on it," I tell Finn, and all my anger comes rushing back. Clenching my fists, I remove them from my pockets.

"Don't give up, man. Look, I have to go." Finn glances at his watch. "Siobhan will kill me if I'm late. We are going cake tasting."

"So she said yes?"

His smile is stretching. "Of course she did."

"You're a lucky man," I tell Finn, and he walks back to me and hugs me. It's quick but tight.

"Thanks, brother." Once he releases me, he leaves.

I walk further away from the house and take out my phone. Ava's phone rings out. When it goes to voice mail, I hang up. What could you say in a voice mail that could start to mend this?

I ring again, and this time, I speak. "I'm sorry for everything, Ava. I want to make this right. Just call me." Not the best voice mail I've ever left, but the most honest one.

I keep walking, knowing I have another call to make, but I don't want to. I need to make up my mind and get my story straight before I ring my da. The ringtone sends my heart pounding. It rings seven times before he answers.

"We need to meet."

"I can't today, but I'll text you a location when I have it." I'm nodding into the phone when he hangs up.

I wasn't going to tell him over the phone that his son was dead. It was a conversation I could only have face-to-face with him. My phone dings and hope surges through me but deflates just as quickly.

What did I miss? It's Darragh.

You got a job in a brothel, Shane beat me up, and Liam raised his voice.

Get the fuck out. I get to work in a brothel? You're having me on. Darragh's message makes me smile.

Yep, you're working with Liam. The decision was made.

I don't think I can accept this kind of punishment. Haha. Fools. Right, check you later.

Stuffing the phone back into my pocket, I'm still grinning as I make my way back to the house.

I need to shower and change my clothes. Entering my room, I'm surprised to find Una sitting on my bed, tears running down her face. My first thought is that he hurt her.

"You were my favorite. You made me laugh. You made me feel like I belonged." Now she looks up at me, and bile churns in my stomach as she points at the hall. "But what you did out there was wrong, Connor. I know this family isn't perfect. I know Shane isn't perfect, but I love him so much."

She's standing now, and I hate her words. "You could have blocked every attack he made. You're stronger, the better fighter, but to push him like that… It wasn't fair." Her voice rises, and I don't know what she wants me to say. "He's damaged enough without you poking at him."

"Don't," I tell her. "Stop right there. You have no idea what you're talking about. You have no idea what he's capable of."

"But I do, and I accept it."

I'm searching her face, looking for the cracks, the lies, but she's firm. I fold my arms across my chest. "Fine, Una. Tell me what Shane is capable of."

She shifts now like she's not so sure anymore, and when I nod, she speaks. "He hurts people. He deals drugs."

I'm surprised she knows that.

"He's killed people." Her voice is so low that I have to lean in, but I heard her right. Now I'm looking at Una differently. How can she lie with him?

But didn't I kill Brian? How could Ava lie beside me if she knew the truth? Would she stay? Would I think less of her, or was this true love? You stand beside your man no matter what crime he commits.

"I'm sorry for what I did in the hall, then."

Una wipes tears from her cheeks.

"I was trying to show you what a monster he was, but you already knew."

The slap across my face stings, and I grit my teeth. That's the first time she's ever done that. Her face is bright red. I'm not sure if it's shame or anger, but she storms from my room. That went well.

I make my way to the bathroom, and the mirror confirms my suspicions about my neck—red marks circle it. A red handprint is bright and visible on my face, and my lip is cut. Swelling has started above my left eye as well. A few days, and they will all be gone. Before I get into the shower, I ring Ava again, and her phone goes to voice mail.

"Just let me know you're okay." Hanging up, I glance back up at myself. For the first time in my life, I can't fight my way out of this, and that scares me more than anything.

CHAPTER TWENTY FIVE

AVA

I'M IN THE APARTMENT, and I've just stopped looking at my phone at this stage. Each time I listen to Connor's voice mail, a lump of ice breaks away from my heart and melts. I love him, but I'm not sure it's enough. A horn beeps outside, and I grab my bag and keys off the counter.

"Hi, Gerry." I climb into the back of the taxi, and my phone rings again. This time it's not Connor. I don't recognize the number. I think about not answering it, but I do in case it's the hospital about my nan. She's getting home today.

"Hello."

"I'm looking for an Ava Smith." The formal voice has me sitting up straighter. Gerry pulls out onto the main road just as I clip in my seat belt. "Speaking."

"It's Claire from Gunnes Auctioneers. I'm just ringing to see if tomorrow is a possible start date for you?"

My stomach erupts with butterflies. A job. I could have a job tomorrow morning. The only thing stopping me is that Connor got me this job. But it would be up to me to keep it. I wasn't going to throw away an opportunity like this.

"Fantastic. What time?" I'm smiling into the phone.

"We open at nine thirty. I'll be here myself and will train you. You come highly recommended."

Guilt sways back and forth in my stomach, but I squash it down. The recommendation not being real doesn't help, but I will prove myself. "That's so great. I'll be there tomorrow morning at nine thirty," I rattle off.

"Perfect, Ava. We will see you then." I end the call and meet Gerry's smiling eyes in the mirror.

"I believe congrats are in order."

"Yeah, just got a job with Gunnes Auctioneers."

His eyebrows rise. "Very swanky." I'm still smiling when I arrive at my old apartment. I don't have much to pack, but I need to get all my stuff out. I'm skittish as I walk up the steps, fear of Brian waiting for me has me pausing and wiping sweaty hands on my jeans. I spend the next few hours packing up my life. A mover is coming for them this evening and bringing everything to my nan's.

Taking a final look around the one-bedroom apartment, I feel the loss for the girl who lived here, the girl who had a job in Smyth's. I miss the simpler times.

I miss Connor. I banish that final thought as I leave the key where I told the moving company I would. I don't want to come back here again. It isn't Gerry who drops me back to Headfort Demesne but another taxi man. When we arrive, there's a man waiting outside my door.

The moment I get out, he introduces himself. "I'm Russell, the landlord. You must be Ava."

Shit, I thought I would be long gone before I had to explain to anyone that I wasn't living here anymore. I give him a tight smile and enter the apartment. I'm still jumpy after Brian, so I position myself close to the knife drawer hold my phone. He ruffles up paperwork as he walks over to the breakfast bar.

"So I just wanted to drop this off to you." Russell isn't how I pictured him. His long hair falls to the center of his back, and as he tucks it behind his ear, I can see leather bracelets covering his wrist.

"Connor covered a year's rent." He's smiling as he tells me the 'good news' but my stomach is in my shoes. "So if you're happy after the year, we can do new contracts. Here's a set of contracts and also the rules. If you want to read through it and sign, then I'll be out of your way." He hands me a pen and turns the contracts around to me. I'm pausing, not sure what to do.

Rent free for a year?

"I have a terrible headache right now. Could you just jot down your address, and once I read through these and sign them, I'll post them back?" I'm used to giving smiles when I don't mean them. People seem to feel like they're genuine. Russell gathers up his stuff but leaves the contracts.

"That's no problem." He's smiling knowing no one in their right mind would pass up an opportunity like this. Once Russell is gone, I don't think but go through the apartment and pack the two bags of belongings I brought here. Leaving the contracts and the keys on the counter, I call a taxi to take me to Navan hospital to collect my nan.

Nan and I are only in her house a few hours when the movers arrive. Nan is so excited to have me moving back in.

"Are you sure, birdy?" She's asked me this several times already.

"I want to be here with you, Nan." She's gives a sharp shake of her head.

"As long as my birdy is happy."

I frown at her words. I'm not happy. My nan being home and safe is everything, but losing Connor took a toll on me that I wasn't expecting.

"Is Connor coming over later?" Nan asks, and I wonder how transparent I am. She always seems to ask the right questions at the right times. I haven't told her about me and Connor.

"He's working," I answer while unpacking boxes.

"That one is a keeper, birdy. I feel it in these old bones."

My throat burns. I thought the same too. But it's funny. Having him and knowing that we started on a pretense compared to not having it all seemed like a no-brainer.

"I'm glad you're home, Nan," I tell her and hug her small frame. She hugs back, her hold strong for a woman of her years.

It's later that night when I'm alone in bed that I take out my phone. I won't ring him, but I don't know... I want to let him know I'm okay without telling him.

Did you hear from the guards about me making a statement? I chew my lip as I re-read it several times. "Just send it, Ava," I tell myself, and finally, my finger hits send. So that's it. It's gone. Nothing happens. No matter how much I stare at the phone, it doesn't light up.

Fine. I lie down and reach for the light switch when my phone lights up. I'm smiling, and a giddiness rushes through me now.

No, Ava, I didn't. But don't worry about Brian. He won't come near you again. Are you okay?

My eyes blur. I want Connor to hold me now and just make this all go away.

I got the job with Gunnes. I hit send and then feel foolish, but I want to share it with him.

I'm so happy for you. You deserve this. Did you hear from Russell? Can we meet?

My poor lip takes more abuse as I re-read over Connor's message.

Yeah, he came around earlier. I better go to sleep. Have to look fresh for this job in the morning.

I'm staring at the phone again, and nothing comes in. I turn off the light and lie down but hold the phone in my hand. I hate how my stomach erupts when it lights up.

You will do great. X

I'm focused on the X, my finger rubbing across it. "I love you," I tell the phone as tears leak out of the corner of my eyes. My stomach cramps painfully, and I pull my legs up into a fetal position. The thought of losing him is causing my pulse to spike. His smile, soft hands, and kind ways torture me. Happy memories haunt me until I fall asleep.

***

The new job is great. I just show people around properties that are for rent. I close three on my first day. Claire says I'm a natural, and it does feel natural to me.

My phone rings when I'm on a break. It's Connor, but I can't answer it. Once it stops ringing, I wait for the message that I have a voice mail. Without fail, it arrives. I'm smiling like an addict as I listen to his voice. Closing my eyes, something burns deep inside me.

"Just checking in to see how the first day went. I know you will do great." A pause *"I really miss you, and it would be great if we could meet up. Just grab a coffee. Whatever suits you."* Another long pause, and I wonder if he's done. *"Let me know."*

I listen to it four more times before I stop acting crazy and put the phone down. I don't respond but finish my day's work, which flies.

Nan has dinner on the table when I arrive home. "It smells delicious," I tell her as we sit down. She's made my favorite of hers—a stew. We eat in silence, savoring each bite.

"Nan, if Jack lied to you about how he met you, what would you do?"

Nan raises her eyebrows and goes to the press under the sink, where she retrieves a box of cigarettes and a lighter. Smoking with Nan is occasional, and when she offers me one, I take it.

"Jack's been gone thirty years now. Your grandfather never lied." Nan lights up her cigarette, and my heart deflates at her words. I was being stupid even thinking of giving Connor another chance.

"But you need to spit out what you're trying to say."

"Fine. Connor lied to me. He met me on purpose to get information out of me." Those are the basics.

Nan takes her sweet time to answer, taking long drags off her fag before flicking the ashes in the sink to her back. I'm taking in the smoke but not inhaling it fully.

"Information about what?" She purses her lips, and I wonder how to explain this to her. But then I decide to just go for it.

"His brother hurt someone, and I witnessed it. So I suppose his brother sent him to find out what I saw."

"And Connor got this information out of you and then left?"

"Well, no. Things actually were going great, and I left when I found out the truth. But Connor never got any information out of me."

I'm staring at the smoke that swirls around the small room. Connor only questioned me at the start, but he never asked after that.

"Maybe you need to talk to the boy and listen to his side of things. No one's perfect, birdy." I put the cigarette out. All it was doing was burning my eyes. Nan is right. I need to at least hear his side of the story.

Once I'm in bed, I take out my phone and text Connor.

I'm free tomorrow if you want to meet up. I hit send and wait. It doesn't take long for him to reply, but his reply isn't what I expected.

A relation of ours died, so I have to go up the north for the funeral. Can we meet up after?

Yeah, sure. Really sorry for your loss.

Thank you. Can't wait to see you. X

I'm smiling again. How easily he makes me smile. I send one final message back.

X

CHAPTER TWENTY SIX

CONNOR

I bide my time slowly and know that it's up now with Shane. He's outside talking to Una. They're smiling at each other. I wait in the kitchen, and when he arrives in, his smile tilts.

"I was hoping I could have a quick word," I say, and he gets himself a cup of tea.

"I'm busy today," he tells me with his back to me.

"Where's Bernard's body?"

The cup smashes on the floor—the reaction I wanted. Shane glances at me over his shoulder, and I can see he's trying to think quick.

"Have you heard from Brian lately?" I ask, taking a sip of my tea, and he's paling and nodding.

"What do you want?"

"Just a quick word." We leave the kitchen, and I follow Shane as he moves swiftly into the dining room. The plaque is like a beacon.

Family comes first.

I always wanted to destroy that plaque, and one day I'm sure I'll get the chance.

"So where is Bernard's body?"

"I don't know what Brian told you, but he's full of shit."

"You get one shot at this, Shane. So I'm going to tell you what I know, and then you can tell me where his body is."

Sitting down. I sip my tea, and I gesture to the seat across from me. When Shane sits slowly, I know I have him by the balls.

"Brian is dead. I blew out his kneecaps before shooting him in the head." I let that sink in. Shane's touching the band on his thumb, and I'm glad he's thinking about Mom. That's what I'm counting on. Whether he really knows what he's doing, he's doing it.

"Bernard was the son of the general of the IRA."

"I know that he was Tom's son and connected to the IRA. I just didn't know that Tom was that high up." He joins his hands now and leans them on the table. "So what, you're going to tell on me? It's my word against yours. Who's to say you didn't kill Bernard?"

I'm smiling at him. It's nearly too easy. "Because Shane, Tom will believe me. I'm his son."

His jaw tightens, and his nostrils flare as he sits back, doubt clear in his eyes.

"My da is waiting on my call to let him know who killed his son. So I can either tell him Brian did it, and that I killed him, or I tell him you did it, and then I have to kill you."

"Mam would never be with Tom."

My composure slips, and I'm leaning in. "Why? Tom never put his hand on her, unlike Michael."

He's shaking his head. "Dad never..."

"He did. But I'm not here to hash that out with you."

Silence descends on the room. He keeps looking at his hands and snapping quick glances up at me.

"Brian was the one who told Harry about the land. I told you he paid off the Gardaí, but you wouldn't believe me. He wanted you out of the picture after you beat him up."

"So you tell Tom—your dad—that Brian killed Bernard, and what? You let me walk away?"

No.

"Where's his body?"

"You need to listen to me. I swear to God, I didn't mean to. It was an unlucky blow."

I didn't need to hear his sob story. My brother was dead. How that happened is irrelevant. When I don't answer but take a sip of my now cold tea, Shane rubs his face.

"At the base of the Loch Leigh Mountains."

The thought of Bernard rotting away at the bottom of the mountains has me looking away from Shane.

"I want him in a coffin, in a hearse that I can drive up the north."

"A hearse. Where do you think I'm going to get one?"

I pin Shane with a stare. "I don't care if you have to buy me one. I will bring my brother home in a coffin."

Shane stands. He's looking a little pale now.

"I'm not finished," I tell him. Clenching his jaw, he sits back down. "In exchange for your life, you'll have to do something for me."

"I'm not agreeing to anything until I hear what it is."

"All I have to do is pick up the phone and say your name, and there will be a bullet in the back of your head. Why don't you get it? You will do what I say." I lean out and let that sink in.

When he doesn't answer me back, I proceed. What I'm about to share with him could get me killed. I lower my voice.

"Mam wasn't killed in a shooting."

Shane's hands turn white as he grips them tightly.

"Tom knew the pathologist who was taking care of Mam." Even speaking about it now is painful. I hate to think of how she really died. "The shooting was staged. She was already dead. Someone broke her neck."

Shane pushes his chair out slightly, the horror evident in his eyes. He loved her as much as I did, so for now, I would give him that bit of respect.

"The fact that someone tried to cover it up meant they regretted it. It was an accident, maybe, but it was also someone close."

"Someone close?" The denial is evident on his face, but when Tom first presented this to me, it took days for me to come to terms with it too.

"Someone must have discovered that she was having an affair with Tom," I say.

"Dad wouldn't hurt her. None of us would."

"I know what you're saying, Shane, and I get that it's painful, but the truth is, someone she knew killed her because they discovered something about her. So my logic asks, who gathers information and sends it back down the line?"

Shane's not going to get this because his mind is stuck on how she really died.

"His informant," I continue, "whoever that is, must have told whatever it was they killed her for. We find him, we find out who killed her."

"But I don't know who he is."

I'm nodding. "But that's your ticket to stay alive. Find out who the informant is, and I'll take care of the rest."

I reach my hand across the table. "Do we have a deal?" His handshake is limp, and sitting with him won't help. He needs time.

"I want Bernard's body here by tomorrow," I tell him, and he looks up at me. His eyes flicker around the room like he just woke up.

"Okay."

***

I spend much of the day packing up my bag. Da texted that we're meeting tomorrow in the same hotel in Monaghan. If Shane doesn't have the hearse ready, I can always come back for Bernard, but telling Dad face-to-face is important. My stomach churns every time I think what I have to do.

A knock on my door has me peering up. Una is half in my room. "Hi."

"What do you want, Una?" I stuff the remainder of my clothes into a rucksack.

"You're leaving?"

I glance up at her. "Yeah, I think I've overstayed my welcome."

The bed dips as Una sits down. "I'm so sorry for putting my hand on you yesterday."

I shrug "It's fine." But it's not. I've lost respect for her. Maybe time will give it back, but right now, I can't look at Una the same.

"It's not fine. I had no right."

"Una, I know you mean well, but I have a lot of shit going on. So…"

Her cheeks darken, and she stands, folding her arms across her chest. "If you need me for anything, just ring."

"Yeah, I'll keep you on speed dial."

"I'm not the enemy here, Connor."

I'm looking up at Una again. "Neither am I. I'm one of the good guys."

Her eyes mist over, and I don't want to make her cry. "It's all fine. We're good," I tell her, but she starts shaking her head.

"No, I know you. I've really hurt you." I tighten my grip on my bag.

"I'll get over it." Una stops me from leaving the room. Her arms tighten around my neck, and I can feel the warmth of her tears on my neck. Dropping my bag, I wrap my arms around her. "Don't cry, Una."

"I love you, Connor," she says to me, and I kiss the side of her head.

"I love you, too."

***

I stay at a hotel that night. I've taken Darragh's Jeep with me down to Monaghan. Shane still doesn't have everything ready, but it will be soon. When I enter the hotel, I notice two men lingering in the lobby. My eyes are more tuned in. Dad sits in the same seat of the bar. I'm not sure if it's lighting or what I'm about to tell him, but he looks older. His eyes are more wrinkled. The embrace he gives me makes me sense he knows the information I'm about to deliver. Otherwise, I would have told him across the phone.

I don't beat around the bush. "I found Bernard."

"I... That's what I thought. He's dead, isn't he?"

"Yes, Dad, he is." His face pinches up as he looks out at the sea of chairs.

"Did you get the person who did it?" Now his eyes burn into mine.

"I did. I gave him a IRA death." His large hand covers mine.

"Thank you, son."

I hate lying, but it's for the best.

"His body will be back up the north by tomorrow. We can bury him then."

"Maybe it's a good thing your mother is dead. This would kill her." Any of us getting hurt would have killed Mam.

"I'll start funeral arrangements." Dad rubs his jaw, and he's aged another five years in a matter of seconds.

"I'm going to head back, and I'll be home tomorrow with Bernard." We give each other a final embrace before I leave. Driving back has numbed me. I want to feel something about Bernard, but all I can muster up is anger toward Shane. I can't seem to find any other emotion.

The hotel room is stark, almost empty. The bed has a floral cover, and the room stinks of cigarette smoke. The thought of staying here for the night alone has me leaving the room. I ring Ava, and I'm actually surprised when she answers.

"Hi." I pause while walking down the hall.

"Hi." She sounds breathless.

"I was wondering if you wanted to meet up now?"

There's a long pause on her end, then "I'm finished in an hour if you want to meet."

"Will I pick you up?" A long pause, and my stomach tightens. She's going to back out.

"Okay."

"Okay." I'm smiling into the phone. "See you soon."

CHAPTER TWENTY SEVEN

CONNOR

I HAVEN'T FELT THIS nervous in a long time. My fingers drum along the steering wheel as I wait across the road for Ava. Everyone seems to be coming out of the office but her. Now I worry she's changed her mind and is holding up inside, or if she's slipped out the back door.

My stomach tightens as she steps out of Gunnes. She looks so good; she looks up and down the street before her eyes settle on the Jeep and then meet mine. Green eyes flare to life, and I swallow the panic that tears through me as she makes her way across the road. I don't want to fuck this up. I lean across and open the door.

"Thanks." She's nervous as she climbs in.

"You look good," I say, and she gives me a tight smile before searching her bag. She hands me a card. "It's a mass card for your friend." I take it, and it feels heavy in my hands.

"It's my brother." I tighten my grip on the mass card.

"Oh, Connor, I'm so sorry." Her small hand touches my arm, and I look at her.

"He was one of the good guys," I tell her, and I swallow the lump in my throat.

"How did he die?" She moves her body so it faces me.

"It was a bar fight. An unlucky blow." I grip the steering wheel.

When she touches me again, I face her. I want to kiss her so much, but her eyes are filled with hesitation the moment I lean in.

"I'm so sorry for lying to you," I say. "But I was going to tell you the truth." She frowns and swallows. "I love you, and I just want another chance with you."

She gazes up at me from under her lashes. "I love you, too, and I want to try again. But I can't bear if you lie to me again."

I pull her into my arms. She hesitates for only a moment before she lets me hold her. I inhale the sweet scent of Ava, and it's home to me. So familiar. "God, I missed you." I kiss the top of her head, and she looks up at me now.

"I missed you, too." When her eyes move to my lips, I don't hesitate to kiss her. Her lips feel softer and warmer than I remember, and I deepen the kiss wanting her so badly right now.

When we break apart, she smiles up at me. "We are in a public place."

"You want to go home?" I turn the Jeep over.

"Actually, I moved back in with my nan."

"If you're happy, I'm happy."

She kisses me softly on the lips. "But we could always use it to meet up, since you did pay rent for a year." Her smile has me pulling away from the curb. The car can't seem to move fast enough.

Once we arrive, Ava actually looks disappointed. "Oh, the keys are inside."

"I have a key from when we installed the new locks," I tell her and open my wallet where I keep the lone key.

"Okay." She's chewing her lip, and I lean across and kiss her. Her hands are on my face, tugging me closer, but it's not close enough. Her skin feels softer as I let my fingers run under her shirt. My touch has her pushing her tongue deeper into my mouth, and I moan.

"Let's go in." She's nodding while reaching the door handle. Her eagerness is matched with my own, and it's not just about having her now. It's hope that we can mend things. My foot kicks the door closed as I move us into the bedroom. A trail of clothes is left behind, and when we reach the bedroom, we're nearly undressed.

My fingers dive down, and she inhales sharply when I push two of them inside her. I want to watch her. My own need grows as her nipples brush my chest.

Each step toward the bed, I remove my fingers before inserting them again. She spreads her legs instantly once she's on her back. My own need soon replaces my fingers, and I don't hesitate as I pump myself inside her. Dipping my head, I take a hard nipple in my mouth, and Ava thrashes under me.

Leaving her breasts, I find her mouth. Our kisses are urgent and wet as I pump harder and faster. Our moans are mingled with flesh hitting flesh, and my release is so close. Ava's face is twisted in pleasure. Taking her nipple between my fingers, I squeeze, taking her over the edge as she covers me with her wetness. I let my seed pour into her before I slow down my thrusts.

I'm kissing her neck and face while trying to catch my breath. "I missed you," I tell her chest, and she shakes under me. When I look up, she's laughing.

"You missed my breasts?" she teases, and her smile is worth everything.

"I did." The answer has her giggling. "They are such beautiful breasts." I touch them, and she hisses.

"They're too sensitive right now."

My body wouldn't mind going again, but I need to slow my pace with Ava.

"Are you hungry?" I ask, placing a kiss on her lips.

"I think so."

I grin at her wide eyes and remove myself from her. "I'll order a pizza."

As I get dressed and make my way into the living room, the emptiness of the apartment shows that Ava doesn't live here. I order the same pizza as before on my phone before putting it into my back pocket. The contracts sit on the breakfast bar, a pen on top of them. She never signed.

I sit around for a bit until she moves up behind me, wrapping her arms around my waist. I cover her hands with one of mine. "It didn't feel right to stay here."

"That's okay. It's here if you want it."

Ava moves around so we're facing each other. "I'm going to stay with my nan for a while."

I wrap my arms around her, and she's tiny in my arms as I look down on her. "Well, we can use it to meet up."

Her cheeks darken, but her lips tug up into a smile. "I think that's a good idea."

"Me too. I might stay here for a while myself. If you're okay with that?"

"Of course. It's your place. But are you not happy at home?"

"It's crowded," I answer, and she laughs.

"I know you live in Whitewood House. It's huge. But you have a lot of family?"

I kiss her on the nose before I speak. "Finn, Darragh, who you met, and Shane." I say his name quickly and can see her flinch. "Also Liam. They're all my half brothers, but my dad is also their uncle." Yeah, this all sounds messed up. "So my other half brother, Bernard, died. I got on with him, and both families don't get on, so I just need some space."

"Sounds very complicated."

"Yeah, it is."

Ava pulls me into a strong hug. "I'm here if you need to talk."

"I know." The pizza arrives then, and I'm happy so we can move away from the topic of my family.

Once we're seated again, I ask about Nan and Ava's new job. Watching Ava talk about her job with such enthusiasm and her nan with such affection, is really nice, and I find myself relaxing more than I have in a long time.

But it doesn't last long as the topic moves on to Brian. "I know I asked you before about Brian, but I just think it's strange that the guards haven't asked me for a statement."

I don't want to lie to her, but the truth isn't something I think she could accept. "I promise you, he will never bother you again."

Ava drops her pizza. "See, what does that even mean, Connor? Does it mean you didn't take him to the guards?"

"I can tell you the truth, but you can't unhear it. So I hope you can just trust me when I say it's over. You're safe." My heart pounds as I wait for Ava's verdict. She chews her lip before she answers.

"I trust you."

Taking her face in my hands, I kiss her. "Thank you." Her saying she trusted me means everything to me. Our conversation drifts back to safe ground, and the day turns to night before we even know it. I forget about Bernard, about my mother's death. I forget about not belonging. Ava makes me feel like I'm part of something. Her smiles are infectious, and my chest tightens at the thought that I almost lost her. Her yawns are growing closer.

"We better get to bed. Are you working tomorrow?"

She's standing and gathering up our dinner that's gone cold. "Yeah, an early rise."

"Me too. I can drop you to work."

"That would be great."

She rings her nan to tell her she's safe as I get ready for bed. I check my phone.

I have everything ready.

It's a message from Shane. I'll bring Bernard home tomorrow, and we can bury him.

"Everything okay?" Ava asks. I didn't hear her enter the room.

"Just thinking about the funeral tomorrow."

She pauses getting changed. "Let me come with you." The idea of Ava with me is tempting, but I'd be bringing her to an IRA funeral. "No, it's fine. It's down the north. But thanks." She looks slightly disappointed as she slips under the covers.

"I love you," I say, and my heart gives a little kick when she says it back. I fall asleep with Ava in my arms, and it's the first full night's sleep I've had in a long time.

***

The markets area of Belfast has come to a standstill. Thousands have gathered for Bernard's funeral. I'm up front carrying his coffin. The Irish flag is covering the coffin, the colors so bright in a sea of black.

I'm front left, along with Seamus and Matt. My dad is on the right with Mark and Joe. The six of us carry Bernard's coffin. As we pass, the streets are silent. The unnatural stillness of the onlookers is a reminder of what we represent for the people.

Some bow their heads in respect. Others huddle their children away from us, like the sheer sight of us might send them down the wrong path. We are the Irish Republican Army. A force that's been protecting the Irish Catholics and trying to take our country back from the British. Our steps are in unison as we make the journey to the Milltown Cemetery where Bernard will be laid to rest in a republican plot.

As we lower his coffin, we pause just above the opening as six fighters step forward, their faces covered in green masks. Their green uniforms pressed and perfect. Guns are armed and fired into the air. Each shot makes my body jump; I keep still on the outside, but inside, my heart beats to the drums that play in the background.

We lower Bernard into the ground and step aside as the priest finishes the funeral. I keep my head bowed and don't look around me. I know the biggest names are here, along with the camera crews. I don't want to be on the front page of the paper.

Once the funeral is over, the crowds disperse.

"Thank you, son." Da walks with his arm across my shoulder.

"He went off with respect," I say.

"Great to have you back, Connor." Seamus falls into step beside me. His weather-beaten face isn't from spending too much time outside. When you lead so many men, it tends to take its toll on you.

"Thank you, sir."

"Are you staying long?" Matt asks.

I glance over my shoulder at him as he walks behind us. He's the same age as me and got on well with Bernard. "Nah, I have to go back." The longing to stay isn't lost in my words.

Seamus and Dad walk together as Matt catches up to me. He offers a smoke, and I take it.

"Fucked up what happened to Bernard," he says as he lights it up. I take the outstretched lighter and light up my own cigarette.

"Yeah, I know, man."

We leave the graveyard grounds and walk with the crowd. It dwindles until only a hundred of us are left, and we make our way into Ronnie Drew. The pub is packed when me and Matt get there. Irish music is being beaten out by a young group of singers.

"Ah, Connor you came back." Molly, Matt's sister drinks from a straw in her glass.

"Yeah, just for the funeral."

She pouts her lips and runs her hand down my suit jacket. "You look like James Bond." She winks, and I smirk at her.

"Jesus, Molly, you're like a dog in heat." Matt scares her off, and we make our way to the bar.

Matt and Molly are Irish twins. When Matt was one month old, his mother got pregnant with Molly.

"Two Guinness," Matt orders, and I have to shoulder and push my way to the bar.

"So what have you being doing?" Matt hands me a pint, and I drink half of it in one go.

"A job for Da." I can't say what it is, and he knows that.

"Shit is going down up here. You're missing all the action."

"I'm sure you can handle it," I say as my eyes clash with my dad's from across the room. "I've got to go. I'll catch you later."

I move through the crowd, and when I reach Da, he leads me to a room out back. Only about ten men are seated. Most of them high up in the IRA Da takes me to a chair in the corner.

"Nothing like a pint at home." Dad raises his pint and drinks it until his glass is empty. "He got a good send off," he says, but I can see the pain in Da's eyes. Pain he won't shed. Maybe he will later on at home, alone, but not here around these men. It would be a sign of weakness. And no matter the loss, you have to only show strength.

"Have you made any progress on your ma?" he asks.

"I will. I have Shane helping me find out who the informant is."

"Shane." Da says his name with disgust. If he knew the truth, Shane wouldn't just get a bullet in the head. He would be tortured.

"Yeah, he fucked some people over, and I found out about it. So I'm using it as leverage."

He nods, but he holds my eye a little longer, and I try to make sure I breathe normally as I pick up my drink. I hate lying to him, but I continue to remind myself that it's what's best.

Da leaves earlier, and the funeral party takes a turn around midnight. The younger members grow wild, and that's when I leave. Walking down Market Street reminds me of how much I miss this place, and when Matt falls into step beside me, I pause and stare up at the stars.

"It's getting wild in there," Matt says. He lights up a fag as I pull out my phone.

I'm staring at the stars. Are you? Once I have it sent, I realize it's three in the morning.

"Shit," I mumble, hoping I don't wake her up.

"What's up?"

"I sent a message to my girlfriend, and I just realized it's three in the morning."

Both of Matt's eyebrows rise. "Girlfriend. I'll keep that one on the down low I can already hear all the hearts breaking." I grin at Matt's over exaggeration.

I was asleep, but I'm out back now. Staring up at the stars. X I'm grinning again.

"Is it dirty?" Matt asks, leaning in. "Staring at the stars? What are you talking about?"

I push him away. **Get inside before you get cold, and I love you.**

My phone bleeps again, and Ava sends me a photo of herself, fresh faced and smiling into the camera. She's standing in the kitchen, and under the image, she's written: **I love you too.**

"She's hot," Matt says. I put the phone away and turn to him, and he holds up his hands. "What?"

She is hot, but I don't want anyone else calling her that.

"Right, I'm off to bed. Will we catch up tomorrow?" Matt sways slightly, and I help him stand straighter.

"Nah, I'm going to head back at first light. But once I'm done down there, I'm sure I'll be home for good." Matt slaps me on the back and walks off. His steps aren't the best, and I watch him until he disappears around the corner.

When I get home, the dark house isn't inviting, and I think about Ava. Maybe I could leave and surprise her, creep into her window. No, she has work in the morning. But going into the house is causing my chest to tighten. The garage is noisy as fuck as I push it open. After pulling the tarp off my motorcycle, I push her out of the garage and carry the helmet. I'll ring Da tomorrow. I don't want to linger around here for too long. It just makes it harder to leave.

Once I've pushed the bike down the road, I jump on and start it up, making the journey back.

CHAPTER TWENTY EIGHT

CONNOR

"**W**HY ARE WE HERE again?" I ask Ava while I balance on the thin walkway that's been laid through a bog and woodlands.

"Please, Connor. Walk properly or you're going to end up in the bog."

I do a little wobble and laugh at Ava. I open up my arms, and she walks into them. I give her a hug. It's beautiful out here. We caught a good day, and being outdoors with Ava is nice.

After leaving Belfast two nights ago, it was six in the morning when I entered Kells, so I did the proper thing and went to Headfort Demesne. I still had notions about crawling into Ava's window. But I left her alone.

Taking her hand, I face forward.

"Thank you." Her smile is wide as we walk. It's funny that we don't meet anyone here. It's like the world has decided to leave us alone.

"So I wanted to ask you..." I stop walking and face Ava again. "We have a family wedding coming up in the summer, and I would love if you came with me."

Her eyes light up, and she's in my arms. "All you had to say was a wedding, and I'm there. Who's getting married?"

"Finn, one of the youngest. We'll meet them before the wedding."

"I really can't wait to meet your family."

"Yeah. I'm dreading it," I admit, and Ava's laughter carries across the land.

"Don't. It will be fine. I'm sure they will love me."

"They'll love you. But I'm not sure how you'll feel about them." The idea of her being in a room with Liam, Michael, and Shane just doesn't sit well with me, but I wouldn't miss Finn's wedding for the world.

"I'll have to get a dress." Ava gives a small, happy clap, and I think maybe it will all be worth it. We spend the rest of the day in the bog and then eating out before going home, where we spend far more time than we intended. Spending our free time together and our nights in each other's arms makes the times I have to go home and interact with Shane easier. I know I have Ava to come back to.

***

The vibration of my phone on the bedside table wakes me up.

"Who is it?" Ava sits up beside me as I turn on a light. Darragh's nanme flashes on the screen.

"Hello ?" I kick back the covers and climb out of bed.

"Connor, I need you now, man."

I'm awake and moving into the living room. "What's wrong?"

"I fucked up!" His slurred voice has got to be caused by more than drink.

"Where are you?"

"Pool house. Yeah, I think the pool house."

I'm back in the bedroom, pulling on clothes, when Ava sits up again.

"What pool house, Darragh?"

"Ours."

Holding the phone away, I give Ava a quick kiss. "Go to sleep, it's just Darragh. He needs a lift. I'll be back soon."

She gives me a sleepy smile before lying back down. "Okay, be careful."

I'm out the door. "Are you still there?" I ask.

"Yeah. Connor, hurry up."

I try to keep Darragh on the phone, but I lose him. I'm in the Jeep trying to ring him back when I get a dead tone. The roads are empty at four in the morning as I speed through Kells. I keep hitting redial, but I still get no answer.

Why has he rang me and not the others?

I arrive at the house, and no lights are on. I turn off my own lights as I make my way around back. The pool house is lit up, and dread snakes it's way around my stomach. Pushing open the door the water reflects the lights back to me, but I can't see anyone.

"Darragh," I call out and can hear movement that seems to be coming from behind the couch. My heart picks up at each step I take, until I'm looking down at Darragh.

There's so much blood covering him, and a blond girl is dead at his feet. "I really fucked up this time, man."

***

FEARLESS #4 IS AVAILABLE FOR NOW: HERE

IF YOU NEVER WANT TO MISS A NEW RELEASE YOU CAN SIGN UP FOR FREE TO GET A NOTIFICATION. HERE

About The Author

When Vi Carter isn't writing contemporary & dark romance books, that feature the mafia, are filled with suspense, and take you on a fast paced ride, you can find her reading her favorite authors, baking, taking photos or watching Netflix.

Married with three children, Vi divides her time between motherhood and all the other hats she wears as an Author.

She has declared herself a coffee & chocolate addict! Do not judge

Social Media Links for Vi Carter

Website

Facebook Reading Group

Facebook Author Page